SHE FELT STRANGELY POSSESSED. . . .

The gleaming eyes that blazed behind the mask had hypnotized her. The male scent of his flesh, combined with the subtle hint of spice cologne, tantalized her and played havoc with her body chemistry.

She wished it were possible to capture this sliver of time—to seal these memories in a bottle like fine wine, to uncork it and savor it again and again. A submissive sigh escaped her. She was losing herself to age-old desires and secret, hungry yearnings. And she wasn't going to fight it—not tonight!

NO EASY WAY OUT

Elaine Raco Chase

A CANDLELIGHT ECSTASY ROMANCE™

Published by
Dell Publishing Co., Inc.
1 Dag Hammarskjold Plaza
New York, New York 10017

ISBN 0-440-16119-3

Printed in the United States of America
First printing—December 1982

To Our Readers:

We have been delighted with your enthusiastic response to Candlelight Ecstasy Romances™, and we thank you for the interest you have shown in this exciting series.

In the upcoming months we will continue to present the distinctive sensuous love stories you have come to expect only from Ecstasy. We look forward to bringing you many more books from your favorite authors and also the very finest work from new authors of contemporary romantic fiction.

As always, we are striving to present the unique, absorbing love stories that you enjoy most—books that are more than ordinary romance.

Your suggestions and comments are always welcome. Please write to us at the address below.

Sincerely,

The Editors
Candlelight Romances
1 Dag Hammarskjold Plaza
New York, New York 10017

NO EASY WAY OUT

CHAPTER ONE

"This is absolutely absurd! It's ludicrous! It's abhorrent!"

"No, it's not. Actually I've never seen the Hollywood Freeway less congested. In fact, we're only forty minutes late. Of course, I wouldn't want to make the run from San Pedro to Beverly Hills every day," Diane answered offhandedly.

"No rational, intelligent person would ever be involved in this travesty!"

"You'll change your mind once you get there. Quimby's estate in the Hills once belonged to a silent-screen star. Thirty-two fantastic rooms, tennis courts, pool, and a view that is breathtaking."

"Diane Stephens, you're ignoring my every word!"

"That's because I didn't bring my Funk & Wagnall's to translate whatever it is you've been saying!" Diane retorted, her lips forming a wide, unrepentant grin. "You know something, Ginger, you sound remarkably like the robots you came here to work on."

"Really, Diane, that is a magnification of the issue.

Stop at the next intersection; the undoubtedly simple solution is a taxi back to San Pedro."

"In that outfit you'll be dragged into the bushes by the first man who comes along," Diane countered dryly. Totally ignoring the preemptive command, she competently guided her VW bug around the knotlike exit ramp that led off the Freeway onto Santa Monica Boulevard.

"Stop complaining." Diane reached out to pat her companion's rebelliously folded arms. "Relax, loosen up, I guarantee you'll have a good time. Halloween comes once a year, and Jerome Quimby's masked costume party is *the* event at AVELCOMP."

"Not being an official employee of AVELCOMP Industries, there is absolutely no reason for me to attend this party. This . . . this disgusting outfit you rented is thoroughly demeaning to a woman of my stature."

"Oh, I don't know," Diane parried blithely, her grinning features illuminated by the amber lights on the dashboard. "Only a woman of your stature could fill that costume out so well." She laughed out loud as a disgusted groan assaulted her ears.

"When you're exhausted with this whole preposterous evening, you'll find me in the car."

Diane expelled an unladylike snort. "You know what I've noticed about you, Ginger? You never use the word *I.* Not only that, but I've come to the conclusion that the reason you haven't got a single wrinkle on your forehead, not a hint of crow's-feet around your eyes, and not one laugh line by your mouth is because you never move any muscles when you talk. It's really amazing. It's like talking to the AV 615."

"The AV 615 is a computer."

"I'm positive the two of you are bloodless relatives," Diane stated in a sober, emphatic tone. "I realize you came here to work on robots, Ginger, but you shouldn't get so carried away that people can't tell the master from the creation." She pursed her lips and exhaled a musical sigh. "Ginger, oh, Ginger, whatever happened to that fun-loving girl I went to high school with in Boise, Idaho?"

"That was years ago. I am now a doctor of physics, an electronics expert, and a mechanical design engineer. And stop calling me Ginger!"

"Oh, pardon me." Diane rolled her dark blue eyes heavenward, her voice dripping with sarcasm. "It is the illustrious Dr. Virginia Farrell, Phi Beta Kappa, Mensa society, and all 'round dull, dreary, boring facsimile of a human being who is sitting in my car."

"Honestly, Diane, you sound the same as you did in the seventh grade. It's time you grew up."

"In some ways I am very grown-up," she announced with smug superiority. "And yet there's a part of me that will never grow up. That's why I love working for AVELCOMP. We get projects from toy and game manufacturers and now, Disney—it's perpetual fun."

Diane stopped the yellow Volkswagen for a traffic signal. Her glittering blue eyes turned to study her friend's impassive features and rigid posture.

"There's something exciting about a costume party and wearing a mask. It brings out all your baser instincts. You feel wild and reckless, daring and wicked. There's even a full moon. Tonight we are really going to howl!" Her low voice lilted off in ringing laughter as she sent the tiny car lurching forward.

"*You* can howl all you want. I'm staying in the car," Virginia Farrell stated coldly. "I refuse to walk in to that party dressed like this. I don't know how you managed to talk me into wearing it in the first place!"

"You put it on because beneath that computerlike brain and armor-clad skin hides the real you. Ready to flout convention, be spontaneous, live dangerously. It's that old Ginger creeping out, ripe for adventure and anxious for action."

Virginia shuddered, her light blue eyes rolling in mute appeal. "I'm beginning to believe you've gone crackers!"

"Ha, ha," Diane yelped, her palm slapping the steering wheel in excitement. "A slang expression! There's hope for you yet." A satisfied hum of pleasure escaped her lips. "When you arrived last week, I couldn't believe the change in you. I was expecting the old Ginger Farrell. The girl who took any dare and welcomed any challenge; the girl who held the record for sitting in detention hall; the girl who was expelled for putting a smoke bomb in the cafeteria trash can; the girl who successfully hid in the boys' locker room and watched the football team shower—"

"That was fourteen years ago," Virginia interrupted with considerable asperity while she wriggled self-consciously against the plaid bucket seat. "You couldn't possibly have expected the same person."

"Well, maybe not as crazy, but certainly not such a . . . a . . . stuffed shirt," Diane admitted with reluctant candor. "When Quimby asked Briarcliff International for a consulting engineer, I never expected an old high school friend to arrive. Gosh, we had such fun together." Diane sighed. "I was hoping it would be like the old days."

"Diane, it's not the *old* days. I've got more pressing concerns than exploding smoke bombs. I came to California to help with design problems your company was having with the Century Three Project for Disney. When those problems are solved, I'll go back to Florida and Briarcliff will send me out on another consulting job."

"You make yourself sound like a piece of equipment instead of a person," Diane grumbled. "It's really a shame the school officials had to discover that the reason you were such a problem was because you were bored and had an IQ of one hundred sixty."

"One hundred seventy three," Virginia corrected automatically.

Diane groaned and rubbed her pert nose in irritation. "That's what I've been trying to tell you, Ginger, you're too damn cerebral."

Virginia couldn't help but chuckle at her girl friend's sudden language advancement.

"I wouldn't laugh," Diane cautioned in a serious voice. "The other day I heard two of our mechanical engineers describing you as a lab coat, glasses, and bun. That's why I picked out that costume. No one will ever guess it's you. They don't think you've got legs, let alone a body!"

"Well, they aren't going to see either the legs or the body," she retorted sharply. "Why couldn't you have picked out something else, like . . . like Minnie Mouse?"

"That would be typecasting," Diane grinned, turning the car onto a posted private road. "You're mousy enough at work."

Virginia moaned and leaned her head against the window. "There is no way I'm getting out of this car."

"I realize that, at five-foot-one, I am ten inches shorter than you, Ginger, but believe me, I'm strong. You are going to the party, and you're having a good time," Diane threatened in a low, deadly voice. "You are dressed like every woman's fantasy; that costume was made for your body."

"What are you talking about?" Virginia shouted, staring at her with wide, incredulous eyes. "My body keeps falling out of this damn costume! You could have picked up another harem outfit like yours. At least all those scarves cover up more than this . . . this . . ."

"The Playboy bunny look." Diane readily supplied the words that refused to be dislodged from her companion's throat. "You look darling. You've got the perfect figure for the costume, long slender legs, a tiny waist, and plenty of . . ."

"But I don't have the personality to carry it off!" Virginia seethed each word through clenched teeth.

"Hmmm." Diane's smooth forehead puckered in resolute concentration, then one blond brow arched delightedly. "You know, with that gigantic brain of yours it seems to me you could be smart enough to play dumb."

"What?"

"It's done all the time," Diane told her cheerfully. "I've seen the most bubble-brained women capture the attention of an entire party by talking and saying nothing that makes the least bit of sense." She cast Virginia a wicked glance. "All you have to do is coo, bat those long mascaraed lashes I created for you, keep licking those hot pink lips, gush, and take lots of deep breaths."

"If I take even one deep breath, I'll be arrested," Virginia replied sarcastically.

"You'll be the hit of the party."

"Diane!"

"Ginger!"

The yellow VW came to a halt behind a queue of cars. Jerome Quimby's Hollywood Hills mansion, a sprawling Spanish-inspired multilevel house, was coruscated in lights.

Towering palm trees and sculptured hedges were cleverly lit with colored spotlights that cast the grounds in eerie, primeval shadows. Ghostly wails, hooting owls, clanking chains, and bloodcurdling screams from a sound effects record knifed through the partially open windows of the parked VW. The perfect accompaniment to the arguing women inside.

Diane drummed five fingers against the dashboard. She decided to try a new tactic. Twisting in her seat, she looked at her friend. "Ginger, when was the last time you had any fun? When all your senses tingled and you felt energized and alive?"

"You know, you're beginning to sound like Lady Macbeth, obsessed not with death but with my popularity."

"You are evading my question," Diane accused in a gentle tone. Her hand touched Virginia's shoulder. "I may not have your IQ, but I can add two and two. You're attractive, intelligent, and have an exciting career. But you're all work and no play, and that Phi Beta Kappa key may be a nice memento, but it won't warm your bed at night. It's better to get hurt occasionally than to become numb from constantly playing it cool and aloof. You're in danger of becoming permanently frozen."

Virginia turned her head away. Her eyes caught the movement of her reflection in the passenger window. My God, she breathed, it didn't even look like Dr. Farrell, the eminent physicist. It did look like a Ginger!

A pair of hot pink rabbit ears was perched rakishly on her shoulder-length brown hair. After a chase around the bedroom Diane had even managed to highlight Virginia's tresses with blond spray, giving it a shimmering, halo effect. Diane had also done her makeup. Skillfully applied, the cosmetics had turned the proverbial plain Virginia into a sultry, sensuous Ginger.

A black bow tie circled her slim throat, and then came an enormous expanse of naked skin. The soft, creamy swells of her full breasts were enticingly exposed while the intoxicating scent of night-blooming jasmine wafted from graceful shoulders and slim arms. On her wrists were wide black cuffs. The rest of her lithe body was poured into a very tiny pink satin costume with high, French-cut legs. Sheer black stockings and black high-heeled pumps completed her provocative attire.

The makeup and exotic costume formed an illusion—a total antithesis of Dr. Virginia Farrell. That woman was a lab coat, glasses, and bun; that woman had the mind of a computer and the feelings of a machine. That Dr. Virginia Farrell wore drab, oversize clothes, no makeup, and cared little about her appearance. That woman was loaned out by Briarcliff International, one of the nation's most famous think tanks, like a piece of equipment.

Dr. Virginia Farrell *was* a boring, dreary, dull nonentity—a passive creature much like an earthworm: miserable, pathetic, creeping along.

A wave of desolation engulfed Virginia. She took a deep breath, then exhaled a long, almost tragic sigh. "The last time I felt a little jolt of excitement was when a ground fault indicator shorted out, and

I got one hundred seventeen volts of electricity circuited through me from the motor I was repairing." Her voice trailed off in a listless whimper; her eyes stared out of the window, searching the shadows harbored by the night for something that seemed to be lost.

Diane moistened her dry lips self-consciously. "Ginger, I'm sorry. I'm not trying to pry or push, but the change in you is extraordinary. I realize we've been out of touch for nearly ten years, but you were so . . . so bouncy and energetic, so . . . so full of life and now . . ." Her hand made a series of loops in the air. "We really haven't had a chance to talk since you arrived. What has happened to you? I remember coming home late from school and my mother telling me you were gone."

Virginia massaged the center of her forehead, her lips twisted in wry self-derision. "Your mother hated me; I'm sure she threw a party the day I left the Davises." She leaned back against the bucket seat with retrospective eyelids closed as visions of the past became more than haunted memories. "Well, your mother was no different from any of the other foster families I was sent to. I was an impossible, rotten brat who kept getting sent back to the children's home. Bill and Hattie Davis put up with me for two years—eighteen months longer than anyone else. And be honest, Diane, during that time I gave you the roughest years of your life."

Virginia slanted an indulgent gaze at her uncomfortably shifting companion. "If the school psychiatrist hadn't found that my problem was intellectual boredom and not willful disobedience, I would have ended up in a juvenile detention center. I'm not proud of what I was or what I did. As I grew older I developed a conscience and the consuming need to change the direction of my life and my attitude." She was quiet for a long moment, reliving all the years of institutional living. An adolescent, angry and alone —for a long time she had hated her parents for dying in a car accident and leaving her with no one. The fear of being abandoned all over again had made her rebel at becoming a part of any family. How much trouble she had caused.

"When you're young, time passes very slowly. Or so I thought until I was placed in an accelerated education program," Virginia recounted in an oddly detached tone. "I was sent to various agencies for extensive testing, placed in college, easily completed graduate school, and got my doctorate. Then Briarcliff snapped me up. I was so much younger than everyone. My only defense mechanism against the barbs and comments was to withdraw, to become a faultless machine, just like the computers and machines I was building."

"Do you . . . do you like your work?" Diane asked hesitantly.

"I really do," Virginia turned her head and smiled, her voice was warm and vibrant. "I even bought a house. It's a Swiss chalet A-frame right on Cocoa Beach. It's all mine, not the bank's. It's my home; I own it. That is important to me." The words tumbled out, vying for importance. "I don't mind living alone—actually I've been alone all my life. I like being sent on different consulting assignments. It's helped with my . . . well . . . my toddler's attention span. The projects I've worked on have really aided people, and I like that too."

"I know; I've read your résumé." Diane was quick to compliment. "Your projects are staggering. Prosthetic limbs, artificial larynges, silicon microchips for pacemakers. You've got every reason to be proud."

Virginia shrugged modestly. "I did some fun things too. Last year I was sent to the Far East to work on audio synthesizers for a toy company. This year I'm creating a legion of lifelike robots and thrashing, snorting dinosaurs at AVELCOMP that will be used in the Epcot Center at Disney World."

"All the things you do are wonderful," Diane said earnestly. "You're a phenomenal success, professionally. But what about your personal life? You've forgotten how to have fun, to relax and enjoy life."

"Maybe I'm doing penance for all the 'fun' I had fourteen years ago."

"Stop talking nonsense," Diane admonished in a sharp tone. "Getting some enjoyment out of life doesn't stop at a certain age and not for a woman of twenty-nine, no matter what her career." She gnawed her lower lip for a moment, came to a silent conclusion, then grabbed a surprised Virginia by the shoulders and gave her a resounding shake. "You are going to turn your life around tonight! You are going to march up those steps and walk into that house and have the best time of anyone at that party. You can do it—think of yourself as Cinderella."

"I wish you had got me her costume," Virginia countered remorsefully. "Look, Diane, maybe you're right; maybe I have been sacrificing my personal life, but couldn't we start out on a smaller scale and with more clothes?"

"No. As I recall, you still 'owe' me one challenge."

"What?"

Diane nodded smugly and opened the car door. "The reason I was so late getting home from school and missed saying good-bye to you was that I was busy plugging up all the water fountains with bubble gum just like you dared me to do." She walked around to the passenger side, pulled open the door, and held down a pair of pink satin ears while Virginia carefully slid off the upholstered seat.

"This isn't going to work," Virginia groaned, hastily restuffing her swelling curves into the bodice of the skimpy costume.

"Bend your head so I can tie on your mask," Diane commanded, wholly ignoring the latter's reluctant behavior. The black silk mask edged with pink lace covered half of Virginia's face. "There, now don't you feel . . . different?"

"Not particularly."

"Ohh . . ." Diane stamped her small slipper-shod foot impatiently. "With that mask on you are totally unrecognizable. Behind that satin shield you can act any way you want: flirt outrageously, kick up your heels, and have fun. Turn this party into your own fantasy world. Just play the coy, wide-eyed, fluffy-headed bunny, and you'll have the time of your life." She flashed Virginia a dimpled smile.

"Now, how do I look?" Diane straightened her tiny blue brocade bodice and twirled slowly for inspection. The rainbow of colorful scarves that formed her exotic harem outfit billowed enchantingly around her petite figure. Her blond hair was pulled into a high, braided ponytail. She attached a pale-blue scarf to a tiny hook on a silver-sequined snood, draped it over her nose so it covered the lower part of her face, and anchored it on another hair ornament. Diane's sapphire eyes glowed with anticipation. She playfully patted the glittering red ruby that was fastened with adhesive tape to her navel.

"You look wonderful." Virginia smiled as they walked up the drive to the dramatically lit mansion. "Diane, if I . . . if I feel too out of place, I'm going to come out to the car."

"Oh, all right." Diane finally relented. "But give yourself a chance, Ginger. Remember, when you open your mouth, don't let anything intelligent come out. If that's too much of a strain, then don't say anything at all. Just bat those lashes, wiggle that fuzzy pink tail, and I guarantee you'll be the bunny of the ball."

CHAPTER TWO

Heavy wooden doors creaked open in response to the summons of the bell. Diane looked inquiringly at Virginia, who gave a casual shrug before proceeding into the dimly lit entry hall. Immediately both women became entangled in tenacious, gossamer webs, courtesy of a large, rather hairy arachnid that was clinging to the ornately carved door frame.

"Both are synthetic," Virginia quickly announced over her companion's loud shriek. She rolled the sticky fibers off her bare skin and helped Diane free herself from the spider web.

The front doors slammed shut with a sharp bang, which caused them both to jump. Two pairs of blue eyes blinked around the large high-ceilinged foyer, which was alive with eerie, moving shadows, courtesy of medieval torches that housed modern flickering amber light bulbs. Music and laughter echoed in the distance, but only three closed doors greeted them. Doors that stood silent as tombs.

"The lady, the tiger, or freedom," Virginia intoned in a dry soprano.

"I told you Quimby *lived* for Halloween," Diane whispered, her eyes darting around uncomfortably. "Mathematically speaking, which door leads to the party?"

Virginia, grinning, cast her a wary glance. "Your guess is as good as mine." Her heels clicked loudly against the marble flooring. She turned the French latch and pulled open an arched oak door.

A bloodred glow illuminated the inside of a large closet and a black casket. The lid of the casket shuddered open, emitting a cloud of ancient soot and then a severed, rotted, flesh-covered hand, which beckoned to the new arrivals. Quickly, forcefully, Diane slammed the door shut.

"Mechanical," Virginia soothed, her lips twitching with amusement.

Diane coughed self-consciously. "I'll open the next one," came her courageous offer. She took a deep breath and yanked open the second door. Her petite body grew inches taller with rigidity. Her words erupted into little squeaks. "Remember that . . . that tiger . . . ?"

Virginia crossed over and peered into yet another closet. A jungle cat was indeed sitting there. Three hundred pounds of pure muscle and stripes. Massive jaws opened to display a vivid expanse of sharp dental work. The feline looked in need of a meal and extremely real.

"It's a hologram," Virginia told her, her tone tinged with respect for their as-yet-unseen host.

"One of the best I've ever seen. Laser beams that project a three-dimensional image."

"Of course it is," Diane cracked, and hastily slammed the door on an exceptionally lifelike animal.

"Process of elimination," Virginia announced, turning the third and final knob. A shower of colorful streamers and confetti covered them amid a triumphant musical fanfare.

"Good evening, ladies."

Both women turned their heads, their eyes rising to focus on a seven-foot gorilla. The furry, perpetually grinning reception committee was bearing a tray of assorted beverages.

"Lead on, King Kong," Diane directed, after taking two tall glasses from among the potent selections. "Here, drink this," she directed Virginia, "it'll calm *your* nerves."

They stood on the threshold of a huge ballroom filled with laughing, dancing, costumed people. The high domed ceiling was lavishly decorated with balloons and streamers in the black and orange colors of Halloween. A large, slowly rotating silver ball sent a shower of stars over the pulsating crowd.

Virginia stared in fascination at the collection of masked, writhing humanity. It was the epitome of a Hollywood movie set: Roman gladiators mingled with cowboys and dance-hall girls while various monsters and outer-space creatures moved their rubber-costumed bodies in perfect rhythm to the music.

Charlie Chaplin was dancing with Mae West.

Harpo Marx duck-walked past, his foghorn bleating a lascivious hello. A hula dancer was demonstrating the latest disco moves to a short, fat man dressed as a bumblebee.

The atmosphere was exciting, electric, and contagious. It permeated Virginia's senses as deftly as the throbbing music invaded her soul. She quickly rechecked the security of her satin mask while her feet carried her farther into the action.

"Notice Julius Caesar?" Diane hissed as she led her past the band toward the crowded bar. "That's Quimby. I'd know that potbelly and bald head anywhere. Talk about typecasting!"

"Just how wild will this party get?" Virginia whispered, her blue gaze deliberately settling on an entwined twosome in a nearby shadowed corner. The woman, attired as a French apache dancer, was determinedly embracing a scantily clad Indian.

Diane followed her line of vision. "Not too wild," she insisted, with a lilt in her voice. "Remember, these masks come off at midnight, and we all have to face one another at the water cooler on Monday morning. Damn," she muttered, "there are two other harem dancers here."

"You outshine them both," Virginia reassured her. "Oh, oh, a cowboy at three o'clock." She hastily gulped down a mouthful of liquor and placed the glass on the bar. The potent liquid soothed her instant onslaught of panic.

"Remember," Diane reminded her, "just coo and flirt."

Without the preamble of an invitation Virginia found herself whisked onto the dance floor by a tall red-haired man in western garb. The band, its members the only people not in costume, had switched to a slower number.

Her black-masked partner tightened his hold around her slim waist. His deep voice drawled intimately into her ear. "You are absolutely the most delectable thing in the room."

"Ohh, thank you," Virginia cooed, her long dark lashes fanning at him through the slits of her mask. She had been worried about following his lead, but it seemed he was content to just stand and rock back and forth to the slow, seductive beat.

"Hmmm, I could just eat you up!" The cowboy favored her with a bone-cracking hug. "What shall I call you?" His hot breath scorched her cheek.

"How about . . . Bunny?" came her affected rejoinder. Virginia licked her pink-tinted lips with the provocative tip of her tongue. Her hands slid down the front of his plaid, silver-studded shirt and adroitly pushed away his warm, hard body.

A low chuckle escaped the cowboy. He deliberately ignored the gesture and let his hands liberally roam over the creamy expanse of her bare shoulders. "You have two of the cutest . . . ears."

Virginia was tempted to tell him that her ears were about a foot and a half higher than where his dark gaze seemed to be lingering, but instead she managed an enchanting giggle. Moments later the cowboy was replaced by an intricately wrapped mummy whose hazel eyes never wavered from her ample cleavage.

Virginia continued to flutter her lashes and babble meaningless inanities. The mummy, however, proved to be a better dancer than conversationalist. On one of his whirling spins Virginia spied Diane dancing close with a broad-shouldered Robin Hood.

The music changed and so did her partner. Virginia was spared flirting with Count Dracula by the necessity of concentrating on the latest disco steps. Her brain calibrated the movements and intricacies of the other dancers, absorbed the kinetics, until she found herself easily duplicating their gestures.

A powerfully built lumberjack used his rubber ax to edge aside the vampire in a bid for her attention. Virginia barely noticed. She had turned the obstacle of learning to dance into a challenge and the challenge into an accomplishment. Her dancing became progressively more uninhibited. Her body was light and buoyant and relaxed, and her mind reveled in this newly discovered world of rhythm.

Virginia was forced to concede that she was enjoying herself and having fun—fun made possible by a hidden identity and a silly pet name. She was feeling more confident every minute, and with that confidence her initial fears and shyness evaporated. The nonstop energy transmitted by the crowd pumped exhilaration into her veins. She cast her wallflower image aside and stepped into a celebration of life.

Reality disintegrated under the music and the laughter and the ever-changing costumed partners.

Fantasy and illusion had become concrete and tangible. The metamorphosis from dull, dreary Dr. Farrell into swinging, uninhibited Ginger was complete.

Virginia laughingly bowed out of the next dance and withdrew to the bar. The bartender, in surgeon's green, whipped up a tall, exotic creation garnished with an array of fruit. She eagerly polished off the innocuous-tasting punch, ordered another, and missed the man's raised eyebrows when she requested a third drink of the beverage he had christened "Kamikaze."

Leaning against the polished oak bar, Virginia searched the shadowy table-lined ballroom and the pulsating crowd for Diane. She discovered her friend at the buffet table. Diane had traded Robin Hood for an Arabian sheikh and was playing her harem girl role to the hilt by feeding her new partner some delicacies.

A red-caped devil plucked the glass from Virginia's hand, wrapped his arms around her waist, and whirled her back among the dancers, never missing a beat of the throbbing Latin tango. For the next few hours Virginia floated from partner to partner. She sampled the smorgasbord, indulged in a variety of exotic libations, and would have made Fred Astaire beg to have her play his leading lady.

She was light-headed, lighthearted, and reckless. Her slightly inebriated consciousness prodded and urged her to be sensible and get some fresh night air.

Once outside, took a deep breath, shook her head to clear it from the music and smoke, and found herself swallowing an unexpected yawn. Suddenly she was glad she had left the madness behind and taken refuge on one of the many balconies that graced the mansion. She looked up into the tranquil midnight-blue sky, lit by a brilliant harvest moon that rivaled the daytime sun.

She leaned against the black wrought-iron railing and became totally mesmerized by the view from Jerome Quimby's hillside estate. At one time the wide sweep of land below had been a Spanish settlement housing eleven families. Now it was an awesome, sprawling megalopolis in a land of earthquakes, where one lived in bondage to the automobile.

To the south was a man-made concrete trail of tied and knotted freeways, spangled with the greenery of palms, leading to the Pacific Ocean. To the north and west lay the fertile San Fernando Valley; in the east, lights from the steel and glass skyscrapers of Los Angeles winked in the night.

Virginia closed her eyes and stretched her bare arms with languid abandon toward the City of Angels. Her lungs were refreshed by the fragrance of exotic evening blooms, while the balmy breeze caressed her warm skin. She had to admit the evening was not the disaster she had expected.

She had listened to countless stories with never a thought to correcting any of the numerous mistakes she had heard. She had giggled enchantingly at the witty jokes, deftly handled the clumsy passes and a few rough, drunken caresses. She had enjoyed playing the uncautious coquette—she was once again an instigator.

Virginia patted the silk mask with sincere affection. It was the catalyst. Behind this mask she felt safe and secure, daring and bold. The tiny, delicate pink satin held back the sane, sensible Virginia and released the heady, flamboyant Ginger. She seemed to be the embodiment of two women—one intelligent, cool, and reserved; the other giggling, flirtatious, and brazen. It was a strange paradox yet not totally an uncomfortable one.

Once again Virginia's light blue eyes focused on the night sky, searching the stars for the constellation of Perseus. There, at the tip of Medusa's Head, was the well-known variable star Algol. Tonight she and Algol shared an affinity among that great infinity that was the universe. Right now Algol sparkled like a gleaming jewel, but in a matter of hours it would grow dim and lose two-thirds of its brilliance.

She too would suffer that same fate. In a few more hours the Halloween party would be over, the costumes and masks put away, and Virginia would once again be a lab coat, glasses, and bun—with an enormous IQ. A rather desolate sigh escaped her pink-tinted lips. Diane had been right: She was missing an integral part of life.

She wondered if some of tonight's brilliance couldn't be harvested and turned into adrenaline that could be permanently pumped into her psyche. It was wonderfully exciting to be treated like a woman rather than a computer or an inanimate piece of machinery. While she might make the feminists wince, Virginia couldn't deny that being a sex object certainly boosted one's sagging ego. It had been a long time since a man had paid attention to *her* rather than her achievements.

But could she change? Tonight was a fantasy, an illusion—it wasn't real. Minute by minute, day by day, that's what counted. Oh, but to escape behind a mask. Virginia wished all women that reward, even if it was for just one night!

Something soft landed against her bare shoulder; her hand came up to capture a tiny pink rosebud that slid against the swell of her breast. Another blossom grazed her arm, then fell silently to her feet. Puzzled, Virginia bent to retrieve it. Her eyes narrowed and focused on a dark shape almost blending into the shadows of the walled concrete steps leading down to the grounds.

"Good evening," drawled a deep masculine voice.

"Good evening," Virginia murmured after a moments hesitation. She watched as he approached, his lean, muscular frame exuding the animal energy and grace of a stalking panther. She hadn't seen him inside. She would have remembered.

He was tall and formidable-looking in his black attire. His broad shoulders and chest were emphasized by a wide-collared, wide-cuffed silk shirt, unbuttoned nearly to the waist, and close-fitting trousers hugged his slim hips. The hard-brimmed Spanish riding hat and black scarf mask succeeded in concealing most of his face, but Virginia could see a straight masculine nose, a strong square jaw and firm, molded lips.

He smiled at her undisguised appraisal, the grooves deepening in his cheeks. "Taking a brief rest from all your attentive partners, my beautiful Rabbit?" he inquired in an amused tone that held more than a hint of a Southern drawl.

She merely smiled. "And you?"

He gave a casual nod, reached up, removed his riding hat and ran a large hand through thick dark hair, distinguishedly streaked with silver. "I'm not one for Jerome's little bashes," he answered dryly, leaning his sinewy body against the railing. "I'm just playing the dutiful houseguest. I rigged up this costume and spent the evening wandering in and out of the main event, enjoying the buffet and the drinks."

Virginia relaxed. He was just a visitor, not an employee at AVELCOMP, so she wasn't likely to run into him at the water cooler on Monday. This information instantly renewed her self-confidence. She felt safe and secure and, suddenly, bold and reckless. Virginia decided to indulge in a little game of feminine seductiveness. She shook back a wealth of hair that shimmered with molten strokes of gold and flashed her companion a provocative smile. "And who are you supposed to be?" Her lashes flirted at him behind the satin mask.

His lips twisted in a little half-smile; his hand captured hers. "A humble bandit of Old California, at your service."

At the touch of his warm lips the skin on the back

of her hand seemed alive with excitable nerve endings. "A very gallant bandit." Her heart pounded roughly against her breast and made her voice quite breathless. "But, alas, I'm afraid I don't possess any jewels that would hold your interest." Her ringless free hand gave a dismissing gesture as she sighed with demure affectation.

The moonlight slanted across his eyes, making them glow like polished agates. His bold gaze held her prismatic irises a prisoner. "Your beauty and charm outshine any gems, fair Rabbit." Again he lifted her hand, this time palm up, his even white teeth lightly nipping the sensitive flesh near her thumb.

The tug of war in Virginia's mind was taking on full-battle proportions. A sensible voice urged her back inside to the safety of the crowd. A reckless entity tempted her to stay and continue this intimate tête-à-tête with the handsome Bandit. Reckless won. Virginia leaned back, hands curved around the railing, one knee provocatively bent, her head cocked sideways in a coy come-hither pose. Her body talked a silent language to his.

"And what do you do at AVELCOMP, my lovely Rabbit?"

She lazily moved one sensuous, bare shoulder. "Oh, a little of this, a little of that." Virginia's smooth, liquid soprano lilted vaguely. "I'm very adaptable." Her iridescent eyes widened innocently behind the flirtatious mask.

"I bet you are." The Bandit leisurely studied her full but lithe, highly visible feminine terrain.

"And what do you do?" Virginia's voice came out an enticing purr.

"A little of this, a little of that. I'm very adaptable too." He had moved closer, his hard-muscled leg casually pressed against her sleek, black-stockinged thigh.

The night air was filled with erotic stirrings. A sultry breeze carried the perfumed offering of evening flowers and deftly blended it with the haunting sound of trumpet notes filtering through the French doors out to the balcony.

The Bandit turned, his voice low and infinitely inviting. "We can't let this music go to waste." His hands slid slowly up the silken length of Virginia's arms to pull her closer.

Her skin tingled with delicious sensations. She leaned forward until her full breasts touched his chest, deliberately teasing the curling mat of dark hairs visible between the parted shirt. Virginia found she was aching to feel the wonders of his firm, athletic body, and her eager fingers curved into his sinewy biceps. The high-heeled pumps added the scant inches needed to put her eyes and mouth on a level with his.

The Bandit's movements were unrushed and sensual. He savored every moment of this encounter. His determined hands slipped down the sides of her satin costume and sculptured her lush curves against his hard frame. She responded quite naturally to the exquisitely pleasurable stimulation he was creating. Their bodies melded together in perfect synchronization with the music.

An undeniable spark of electricity flowed. Time and circumstance prevailed. Barriers were lowered, reserves set aside, as were the rules. They were two puppets in Fate's scheme. Puppets whose strings were controlled by surging emotions and heightened desires.

His caressing hands blazed an erotic trail down her spine to the rounded contours of her buttocks. There his fingers tangled and played with the fluffy white bunny tail. Her hands explored the steel strength beneath his shoulders; her fingertips gently massaged his neck, then moved upward to his face. Pastel-pink fingernails traced the angle of his jaw and the curve of his lean cheek, teasing the lobe of his ear before they submerged themselves in the virile coils of dark hair that curled onto his shirt collar.

Virginia had succumbed to a world hidden deep within the secret recesses of her female psyche. A world controlled by sensual pleasure. A world sharp and alert with a brilliant burning. Her mind felt strangely possessed. The gleaming eyes that blazed behind the black scarf mask had hypnotized her. The inherent male scent of his flesh, combined with the subtle hint of spice cologne, tantalized her libido and played havoc with her body chemistry. She luxuriated in the masculine physique that enveloped her like a second skin.

She wished it were possible to capture this sliver

of time—to seal these memories in a bottle like fine wine, to uncork it and savor it again and again. She was losing herself to age-old desires and a secret, hungry yearning. She wasn't going to fight it—she was going to enjoy it. A submissive sigh escaped her. Virginia snuggled contentedly into the warm hollow of his neck, her body burning its womanly imprint into his hard, slim, masculine form.

What had started out as fun and games beneath the harvest moon suddenly flared into desire. Desire that was sparked and fanned by the golden-haired temptress the Bandit held in his arms. The smooth expanse of her bare skin was like velvet beneath his palms. Her supple anatomy responded to his every direction. Her eyes mirrored hidden pleasures; her perfect lips tempted; the subtle nuances of her perfume seared his brain. The total impact of her femininity rendered him intoxicated and irresponsible.

His knuckles stroked the delicate hollow beneath her cheekbone, then flowed down the sensitive tendons of her throat. She moved her head, sending silken waves spilling over his arm, and allowed his questing fingers free access to the erogenous terrain exposed by the brief costume.

The Bandit's long fingers captured Virgin 's face. His lambent gray eyes studied her glowi al features in the luminous night. "You ar
His voice was a hoarse whisper. His
the outline of her half-parted lips, th
possessive mouth filled a sudden g

His probing tongue was insistent, penetrating into the lush interior of her mouth. She met it, hesitantly at first, then with matched fevered passion. Their tongues worked together like skilled swords, thrusts and parries, ripostes and lunges—a well orchestrated intimate duel.

Time dissolved into delicious slow motion. They explored each other with hands and fingers, mouths and tongues. The delicious sensual stimulation each gifted the other with only enhanced their mutual pleasure.

His palm stroked the meager satin cover from her swelling breasts. His rough fingertips tenderly found, then teased, her excited nipples. Her responding whimper of pleasure aroused him.

Instead of pushing the Bandit away Virginia arched her back and guided his dark head lower, silently urging his lips to replace his conquering hand. The lash of his tongue against her sensitive peaks sent sweet sensations effervescing through her blood. Primitive passions carbonated and exploded under the erotic magic that surrounded her.

This was madness, her mind shouted. You don't even know this man! But that only heightened Virginia's ecstasy. Sanity's voice drowned beneath the blistering rush of wild heat surging through her body.

Her inquisitive fingers pressed into the working muscles of his back and shoulders. She felt him quiv- [illegible]ith pleasure when her teasing tongue traced the sensitive curves of his ear and her teeth tugged lightly at the lobe.

His insistent mouth found its way home to plunder her eager lips. His hungry kiss absorbed her very breath and made her gasp and shudder against his virile frame. Her soft breasts were crushed against his hair-roughened chest and the friction of hard flesh against silken skin gave her instant gratification.

From inside the house came the deafening sound of Big Ben striking the witching hour: a sound that reverberated and invaded their private world of pleasure. At the twelfth chime Virginia found herself released. Suddenly shy, she turned away and hastily restored her twisted bodice.

The Bandit's hands slid around her waist and pulled her back against him. "Now we can get rid of these damn masks." His voice was ragged as his lips nuzzled her ear. "I want to see what you look like, my passionate Rabbit."

Her body temperature dropped ten degrees, and her pulse rate and blood pressure plummeted below life-sustaining levels. Remove her mask! Virginia froze; her mouth went dry; her muscles tensed. Why, she'd sooner take off her costume and stand before him completely naked!

It may be irrational. It may be insane. But the mask was her shield, her protection. Without it—without it this fantasy would end, this passionate woman would cease to exist. Names would be applied to faces. The magic would end. She didn't want that. She wanted to sustain the illusion—to postpone reality.

She was suddenly cold sober and completely sensible. All right, mental wizard, Virginia challenged herself. Think of something. Think of a way out of this mess. Think of a way to be safe and free.

Virginia turned in the Bandit's arms, her eyes gleaming in the moonlight. "Why don't we make a little game of it." Her voice caressed him with coy persuasion while her fingers walked a titillating path across his bare chest to the base of his throat. At his arched brow Virginia gave a light flirtatious laugh and pulled him toward the balcony railing. "Untie your mask, but don't turn around until you count to five."

"All things considered, don't you think this is a little silly," came his dry rejoinder.

"Oh, darling Bandit, it is a party." She fluttered her lashes and pouted prettily. "Humor me, please."

He sighed and gave a resigned shrug. "All right, honey, but I'm a fast counter."

Virginia gave him a warm smile and pressed a quick kiss at the corner of his handsome mouth. Her last smile was the brightest, the last kiss the sweetest.

She moved to stand behind him, carefully edging back toward the marble staircase that led to the grounds. She watched his fingers move to unknot the scarf mask, then she slipped off her high heels, turned, and silently fled down the steps.

Her feet were swift, sure vehicles carrying her

down the twisting incline. Bramble bushes reached out and snagged her body as if to block her escape.

Virginia heard his shout and quickly increased her speed. The queue of cars loomed before her like a massive metal serpent. She ran in the direction of Diane's yellow VW, crouching low when she heard the ringing of the Bandit's shoes on the pavement and the increasing anger in his voice. Bumpers and fenders shielded her from his view; her stockings were tattered silken threads that were welded to her perspiration-soaked legs.

Virginia sneaked a look and relaxed when she spied the Bandit's tall figure turn and run in the opposite direction. Quickly she pulled open the car door and slithered into the cramped backseat. She yanked the bunny ears from her hair and pulled an old blanket over her trembling body. Here she lay, uncomfortably curled on the tiny seat, gnawing her lip till it bled, and praying the Bandit would give up his search.

CHAPTER THREE

"I've brought my own coffee. I've tasted yours," a disgustingly cheerful voice announced.

A pair of bleary, mascara-glued eyes squinted in hurtful contemplation at the shining stainless-steel percolator. Virginia stumbled over the rumpled foyer rug and fell against the door. Her swollen tongue tried to moisten a mouth that tasted like a million Q-Tips. "What . . . what time is it?" The words irritated her vocal chords.

"Nearly noon," Diane Stephens answered promptly. She strode across the darkened living room and broke open the tight cocoon of drapes, letting the lilac walls bloom in the sun. She eyed her friend's twisted, inside-out wine cotton housecoat over misbuttoned matching pajamas with amusement. "Ginger, you're going to have to party more often; no one gets hangovers anymore." Her tongue clicked against the roof of her mouth. "Come on, girl, a couple of cups of caffeine will perk you right up."

Virginia pushed her tumbled brown hair back off

her face. Her fingers stuck to the strands and came away streaked with spray gold. She groaned loudly. "I feel like death warmed over." Her bare feet shuffled a path through the white shag carpet into the dining room. "It was all those Kamikazes. The Japanese could've won the war with that drink." She collapsed onto an antique pink side chair, yawned, then closed her eyes. The blond, red-jump-suited figure continued to dart in and out of the kitchenette clanking cups and spoons.

Diane wriggled into an opposite chair, slid one steaming cup toward Virginia, and lit a cigarette. "Well?"

"Well what?" A pair of dull, iridescent blue eyes peered into the aromatic liquid and tried to find ambition and comfort in the dark depths.

Diane made a hissing sound. "I've been on pins and needles for the last eleven and a half hours. You were tight as the proverbial clam last night. I want to know why you were hiding in the backseat of my car." She sucked in a lungful of low tar and nicotine smoke. "I want to hear everything."

"Everything?" Virginia shuddered and drained her coffee in three burning swallows. She held out her mug for a refill and drank the second cup more cautiously. Caution, she winced in silence. What happened to that last night?

"God, Ginger, you can be maddening." Diane counted to ten, sipped her coffee, and tried another approach. "I was watching you. Don't try to tell me you weren't having fun last night. That wasn't why you ran."

"No." Virginia exhaled forcefully and rubbed a weary hand over her drawn features. "That wasn't why I ran." She leaned against the ladder-back chair frame and took a deep breath. "You're right, I was having fun, more fun than I've had in a long time—a lifetime," came her truthful confession.

"Tell me what happened."

"I needed some air, all that smoke and the music and the noise. I was out on the balcony when *he* appeared."

"He, who?" Diane straightened attentively, her dark blue eyes wide and bright.

"The Bandit. He said he was Quimby's houseguest," Virginia explained. Her fingers drummed thoughtfully on the pink antique table. "Didn't you see him inside?" she asked. "About six foot, dressed in black with a scarf eye mask and a Spanish riding hat?" Her voice slowed and became more expressive. "Nice straight nose, smoky blue eyes, silver wings of hair at his temples." Virginia's eyes shifted to stare at the oriental wallpaper, her cheeks taking on a stain of ruby wine. "Broad shoulders, deep voice, great after-shave and the most sensuous mouth." A soft musical sigh escaped her lips.

"I wish I did," Diane echoed that sigh. "So?"

Virginia looked at her and blinked. "So what?"

A short scream pierced the room. "You are so . . . oo dense! What happened on the balcony that made you run?" She stubbed out her cigarette and tapped the cellophane pack for another.

"The balcony, the balcony . . . that damn balcony!" Virginia's voice rose in anger and self-condemnation. She wiped her damp palms together. "What happened on that balcony was a combination of too much moonlight, too much fantasy, too many drinks, and too many smoked oysters!"

"No kidding," Diane breathed. "Right on the balcony!"

"Don't look like that!"

"Like what?"

"Like the ecstatic fairy godmother from Cinderella," Virginia retorted harshly. She pushed herself from the chair and restlessly prowled around the room. "I feel cheap and disgusted and embarrassed." Her index finger stabbed the air. "What's worse, I feel so stupid for running."

"Why did you?" Diane asked, her curiosity momentarily overriding her acquisition of yet another filter-tipped cigarette.

Virginia dropped back into the chair. "Midnight chimed and . . . and the Bandit wanted the masks off." She hid her face in her hands, her voice muffled. "I couldn't . . . I just could not take off that mask." Her hands fell heavily against the table. "I don't know. There I was, necking and petting and being totally uninhibited with a stranger in the moonlight—that damn costume was half off—but when it came to that tiny scrap of a satin mask—no! I couldn't take it off." Virginia's glum expression focused on Diane. "I ran like hell off that balcony."

"God, Ginger, don't you think everyone felt stupid and embarrassed? You should have seen all the sheepish, mottled faces when those masks were peeled off." A burst of giggles erupted from her throat. "The guy in the bumblebee suit turned out to be Frank Webb from the engineering library!"

Diane tapped Virginia's nose. "My guess is that you were more confused by your overactive hormones than anything else." The ensuing silence confirmed her pronouncement. "Ginger, you should take a break from reading *How to Split an Atom* and start dipping into the best sellers. *Nice Girls Do* turn into *The Sensuous Woman* and *Every Woman Can* learn *How to Make Love to a Man.* It has nothing to do with moonlight and aphrodisiacs. So you played slap-and-tickle with a stranger on the balcony. You don't have to be ashamed of that. Men are all for aggressive women these days."

"But that wasn't me!" Virginia returned, her voice high and forceful. "I'm not like that. I'm . . . I'm . . ."

Diane interrupted her stuttering. "We're all like that. All it takes is the right man, the right moment, the right surroundings. For God's sake, you're carrying on like some Victorian virgin." She stopped and eyed the lowered head in wonder. "Ginger, you aren't a . . . are you?"

"No," came a dull voice. "The momentous occasion took place in the back of a van during my junior year in college. It wasn't a big deal; in fact, the anticipation was better than the actual event."

"But things got better?"

Virginia's direct gaze pinned Diane. "Look, I am not very good with men. I am not very good with people. Give me machines; at least you know where you stand. It's either on or off, and when it's on, there are no surprises."

She took a deep breath, then answered Diane's unspoken question. "It was in graduate school. I was madly in love with Cal Jacobs. We were working on our dissertations. I made it, he didn't. Briarcliff picked me, not him. Everything fell apart. Jealousy replaced love, if love was what we had.

"A man seems to have a difficult time accepting a woman who surpasses him educationally, intellectually, and monetarily. I have more fingers than I have had sexual encounters. I guess I am still a virgin."

Diane eyed the two cigarettes burning in the ashtray, grimaced, and stubbed them both out. "Somehow I thought it would be easier for a woman like you. You meet so many men, travel to exciting places, have a highly respected job. You're earning a fantastic salary. I thought your life would be just a whirl of erotic, stimulating encounters."

Virginia gave a humorless laugh. "I wish it were. It's me. I've always been a loner, and when you're alone, every emotion echoes louder. You learn to control those echoes."

"How loud did the Bandit make your emotions echo last night?"

"They screamed," she confessed. "He was . . . he was slow and easy and confident and experienced." Her mind instantly replayed the erotic highlights of her balcony tête-à-tête.

Virginia could feel the strong fingers that had caressed the supple length of her spine. A warm rush of heat washed over her skin. Her breathing became labored, and she swallowed convulsively, trying to ignore the tingle in her breasts.

"He made me feel like . . . like the most desirable woman in the world. If he had asked, I would have gone to bed with him." Her eyes followed the intricate rose pattern on the stainless-steel spoon.

"That's a healthy admission." Diane grinned as she refilled the coffee mugs.

"Last night was physical. We were two strangers who overreacted to the fantasy of the evening," Virginia countered, her voice and features quite serious. "We became our costumes, and I'm no Playboy bunny."

"Listen, Ginger, last night turned out to be a very important turning point for you. For once you were not a glass of water: colorless, odorless, and tasteless. You were . . ." Diane picked up the spoon and tapped the white china cup. You were like coffee: rich, aromatic, exotic—and stimulating. Now tell the truth, don't you feel the better for it?"

"The only thing I feel good about is knowing that the Bandit does not work at AVELCOMP."

"Why did that sound more like a moan than a cheer?"

"All right, maybe I am a little sad," she admitted with obvious reluctance. "Yes, last night was erotic and stimulating, and I felt . . . I felt more like a woman. But it was *all* fantasy, Diane," Virginia stated evenly. "I deal in reality, and I am absolutely positive that I could never repeat last night's performance."

"A strictly enforced diet of reality is very bland, very repressive." Diane sighed. She studied her poppy-tinted fingernails for a long moment, closed her eyes, and smiled. "Ginger . . ." The blue eyes opened and energetically focused on her victim. "I am going to make sure you don't leave California the same way you arrived. I am going to spice up your life if it kills the both of us."

"Diane, please—"

"You will thank me, I promise," she continued in her rapid staccato. "We'll start out slow . . . we can change your image by steps rather than leaps."

Diane's gaze drifted around the elegantly decorated apartment. The lilac-tinted walls deftly blended from one room to another. A white curved sofa and chrome-and-glass accessories dominated the living room, while a harmonious mix of refinished antiques and oriental touches complemented the dining area. "You know, I'm really glad you got Joan Scoville's sublet. She's a fantastic interior designer, and this place certainly strokes one's morale."

"Diane, if you think your steamrolling tactics are going to work on me again, you can just—"

"Ginger!"—she affected a shocked position with

the back of her hand against her forehead—"you wound me. I've never met any more effective steamroller than yourself during our high-school days." Diane grinned and flashed her a disarming smile.

"Run along and take a shower and shampoo that spray paint out of your hair. I'll fix us some lunch, and then we can spend the rest of this glorious, sunny day shopping the boutiques in the Port of Call Village. I saw the inside of your closet last night; your wardrobe needs help. A few new blouses and sweaters, better fitting slacks, and—"

Virginia's loud, painful groan was smothered by Diane's continued tirade. With a resigned sigh she pushed herself away from the table and shuffled toward the bathroom. It was useless to try and stop a steamroller, especially one with a loving heart.

The Santa Anas were blowing—strong, dry, and hot off the Rockies. The winds mixed with the sun and the auto fumes to spread a cloying blanket of grit and smog over Los Angeles and the commuter-congested freeway. The winds made everyone restless and uncomfortable, provoked tempers, sapped energy, and dampened creativity.

Virginia cursed that hellish Monday sixteen times before noon. She tossed her third and final lab coat into the laundry bin. The first had been splattered with hot solder, the second was soaked with a phosphorus doping solution, and this one still sizzled from arsenic burns. The day was definitely jinxed—and it had started the minute the alarm had gone off.

In her haste over breakfast she had neglected to put coffee grounds in the percolator, and after her shower was greeted by a steaming cup of water. Her hair normally stayed in a neat, controlled topknot, but this morning it had defied the strength of four rubber bands and two-dozen bobby pins. The obstinate thick brown waves refused to be coerced into anything but a side-parted pageboy.

If that hadn't been enough—Virginia snorted as she reached for a rubberized chemical apron—she felt ill at ease in her new clothes. The tailored brown-and-white-striped oxford cloth shirt defined her full breasts and slim midriff, while the narrow khaki twill pants encased smooth hips and long legs. They were just part of a sleek designer wardrobe purchased on her Sunday shopping spree. Diane had made sure she didn't go back to her loose blouses and baggy slacks by depositing them in a Salvation Army canister.

The new outfit had already caused her an embarrassing moment in the company parking lot. She had bent to retrieve textbooks, manuals, and an attaché case from the rear seat of her rented beige Ford Fiesta. One of the young, gum-chewing mailroom clerks walked by, whistled, and muttered, "Very nice, babe."

Virginia's palms followed the rounded contours of her backside. "Very nice, indeed," she muttered gruffly. She was not at all comfortable with the image her new clothes projected. Her only consolation was that she was the sole occupant of the electrochemical lab. The office staff rarely ventured through the ultraviolet-lit air lock into the contaminate-free "white room."

With her sleeves rolled up and shield gloves protecting her hands, Virginia secured long-handled forceps to lift a vial of liquid helium from a pressurized storage container. Using a special insertion hook, she extracted a cryotron chip from its minus-four-hundred-degree environment, then quickly returned it to the receptacle before rime frost occurred.

The cumbersome gloves were discarded and magnifying glasses put in place, and she carefully plugged the tiny electronic device into the socket of the printed circuit board. The one-tenth-inch piece of silicon could switch a circuit on and off as many as one hundred megacycles per second in a computer.

Virginia returned the PC board to a special copper cold-pack unit she had developed and slid it into the computer software package. If all her testing and evaluations were correct, this would solve one of the problems AVELCOMP was having with the software.

So engrossed was she in charting the visible wave patterns on the oscilloscope's fluorescent screen, Virginia failed to realize that she was no longer alone in the lab.

"Dr. Farrell, I'd like—" A nasal voice jarred her concentration. Startled, her pencil and clipboard clattered to the floor. Virginia straightened and found Jerome Quimby's pudgy face looking even more bloated through her magnifying glasses.

"I'm terribly sorry, Doctor." Quimby ran an anxious hand over his bald head. "I didn't mean to interrupt." The short, stocky president of AVEL-COMP nervously tugged at his gray plaid vest. His dark gaze drifted toward the continually pulsating waves on the scope.

"Your flip-flop problem has been resolved," Virginia told him. She lowered the magnifying glasses slightly to massage the bridge of her nose. "I'll type my report and make a detailed schematic of the copper-nitrogen vacuum process for your staff. I can begin work on the tactile sensor system the day after tomorrow."

Jerome Quimby stared at her for a long moment. Then his thin lips curved into a blissful smile. "Congratulations, Doctor." His beefy, moist hand clasped hers. "We've been banging our heads against the wall for three months, and you conquer the problem in just one week. You people at Briarcliff certainly live up to your reputation as wizards." His hazel eyes looked past her. "Well, Alex, between the two of you, I doubt we'll miss a deadline."

"Your facilities are very impressive, Jerome, as is my learned colleague," a masculine voice intoned from the rear equipment bank.

The distinctive deep baritone with more than a hint of a Southern drawl kindled an erotic memory and simultaneously sent a wave of nausea washing over Virginia. It couldn't be him, could it? But that voice? She took a deep, steadying breath, turned, and was instantly thrown into a panic—it was the Bandit!

Virginia's eyes became fixed on the advancing

masculine figure that loomed larger than life through the aggrandizing lenses. There was no mistake. Today his animal energy was contained in an impeccably tailored navy business suit, but her fingers tingled under the remembered intimate exploration of the hair-roughened flesh hidden beneath his light-blue shirt and tic-weave jacket.

Without the scarf mask his rugged, bronzed features were even more handsome and compelling. His eyes glittered like diamonds and echoed the silver strands that winged at the temples in his dark brown hair.

While Virginia mentally acknowledged the delayed Halloween unmasking, the Bandit seemed totally oblivious to her identity and interested only in the lab. She decided to make his ignorance work to her advantage. After all, he had met Ginger, not the perfunctory, diligent, remote Virginia. And that was exactly whom he was going to meet!

Jerome Quimby's sharp tones penetrated the exaggerated silence. "Dr. Virginia Farrell, this is Alex Braddock from SoLas Incorporated. Alex is here to work on the robots too. He'll be sharing the lab."

"SoLas?" Virginia inquired in a curt tone. Her index finger pushed the magnifying glasses back in place, knowing the distortion would aid her disguise. "Isn't that the solar energy and laser group out of New Orleans?" Rudely she slid her hands into the rubberized apron's pockets and acknowledged the introduction with a regal nod rather than the customary handshake.

"That's correct." Alex flashed Virginia an expansive grin that went unreciprocated. He gave an inward grimace. It seemed Dr. Farrell was one of those scientists who felt a personal affront whenever they had to share a facility. He looked through her bifocal lenses into a pair of unadorned, blinking eyes and was suddenly reminded of a frog he had once dissected in biology.

"This is the third time I've been privileged to work with a member of Briarcliff. Always very successfully, I might add." Alex tried flattery, but it too failed. His gray eyes eagerly left Virginia's nondescript, stoic features to focus on a bay of unfamiliar instruments. "What is your field, Doctor?"

"Cryogenics," she told him in a superior voice.

"Dr. Farrell is one of the nation's leading cryogenic physicists," Jerome Quimby offered. A bubble of laughter erupted from his barrel chest. "I think it's rather ironic to have a solar technician who deals with heat energy quartered with a physicist who deals with freezing."

"Science is known for such diametric viewpoints." Virginia's tone held a wealth of patience. She knew from a Briarcliff briefing that while Quimby headed one of the country's leading electronic-computer laboratories, his forte was in management and selective hiring. He possessed only a rudimentary knowledge of engineering.

Virginia silently suffered through Jerome Quimby's nasal dissertation on the laboratory's obvious features. Her gaze drifted back to Alex Braddock's chiseled profile. Her eyes explored the planes and angles of his face and followed the poetic pattern made by his dark wavy hair.

The carnal memories of their balcony liaison flooded back to both haunt and excite her. Despite the air conditioning the crisp, tangy scent of his cologne made her nostrils flare. Her breathing came faster and heavier when she focused on the movement of his lips. Her toes curled inside her crepe-soled, tan leather oxfords as she followed his gesturing hands.

She reined her thoughts sharply. She had to get him out of the lab. She needed time. Virginia surreptitiously slid her hand along the formica countertop until it came in contact with the computer terminal. Her pinky hit the ring key. A moderate-pitched tone alarm sounded.

"Doctor"—Quimby sucked in an apprehensive breath and lifted his hand from the humming printer —"did I . . . did I do something?"

"I certainly hope not," Virginia returned in a brusque monotone. Her skilled fingers expertly typed a message on the keyboard. Instantly the printer responded by bursting into a loud, lengthy typing operation. The resulting noise effectively ended any further conversation. "I'm afraid I must get back to work. Excuse me, gentlemen," she said, raising her voice, then turned to randomly adjust knobs on the scope.

"Certainly, Doctor," Quimby yelled over the din, giving Alex a helpless shrug.

She favored the departing men with a preoccupied wave, held her breath until they disappeared behind the air lock, then quickly punched the terminal's escape key, shrouding the room in blessed silence.

Virginia's head collapsed into her hands, and the magnifying glasses slid down her nose and clattered against the stark gray tile. Numb fingers attempted to rub the strain from her forehead, but her subconscious echoed the problem of Alex Braddock, alias the Bandit, in an ever-increasing distressing refrain.

A clenched fist punished the countertop. Why had she ever agreed to go to that damn Halloween party? Why had she worn that suggestive costume? Why had she perpetrated the illusion by pretending to be what she wasn't?

The whys combined with the heavy apron to crush against her chest. She felt trapped and smothered. Her skin prickled with invisible sensations; she scratched her arm until it was red and bumpy.

"I need help!" Virginia's unnaturally high, strained voice ruptured the quiet. "Diane!" She quickly untied the apron and threw it on a nearby table.

Virginia ran to her desk and made a grab for the telephone. Her frantic fingers and perspiration-soaked palms sent the entire mechanism crashing to the floor.

She closed her eyes, took a deep breath, and tried to get a firm grip on her frazzled thoughts. A decade-old demon surfaced and humorously reminded her that this was like old times. It was no different from the predicaments she had got herself into during high school.

I handled those easy enough, Virginia thought with cocky assurance. Alex Braddock didn't flick an eyelash over me. I fooled him.

Feeling relaxed, confident, and in control, Virginia decided to call Diane and laugh at the problem over lunch. She bent over to retrieve the telephone.

"Oh, Dr. Farrell—"

Alex Braddock's mellow tones caught her off-guard; the receiver slithered from her hand. She swallowed and turned her head toward the door. "Yes?"

His gray eyes locked onto a pair of wide sapphire orbs, and a glowing face surrounded by a silken tumble of brown hair. His gaze moved on to trace the totally feminine anatomy. From the symmetry of her full breasts the supplely arched back to the rounded derriere—this appeared to be a wholly different woman.

Virginia clamped viselike fingers on the elusive telephone and quickly straightened. "What was it you wanted, Mr. Braddock?" Her own face mirrored his enigmatic expression.

"I have some equipment arriving later this afternoon," Alex told her politely. "I hope to keep the disruption to your work at a minimum."

"That's most considerate," Virginia returned with a curt nod. Under his steady gaze she began to fidget uncomfortably. She coughed and looked pointedly at the telephone still clutched in her hands. "Was there anything else?"

"Not right now." He gave her a wide grin before disappearing into the air lock.

CHAPTER FOUR

"Spinach salad is the perfect tranquilizer." Diane exhaled a smug, triumphant sigh as she and Virginia walked across the employees' parking lot. "You see how easily everything is explained? You've upset yourself for absolutely no reason."

"You've explained it easily, but *I'm* still unsure." Virginia shook her head, then impatiently looped thick brown waves behind her ears. "I thought I fooled Alex until he came back to the lab." A cold shiver zigzagged down her spine. "If you could have just seen the way he kept staring at me."

Diane struggled to open an oversize steel door. "Even with your new clothes and your hair loose, you don't come close to my creation of Halloween night," came her breathless rejoinder. She scooted into the air-conditioned building, leaving the heavy door to hiss closed. "You just overreacted," she stated with dogged determination, then cast a sidelong glance, "or were you, perhaps, indulging in some wishful thinking?"

Virginia leaned against the green painted concrete

wall, her eyes drifting aimlessly around the empty service corridor. "Maybe you're right about both those statements," she admitted in a reluctant, subdued voice. "Alex Braddock was very complimentary, very easygoing, and very personable. I came off the classic ego-inflated bitch." Her voice hardened, and her fist punched the porous block wall. "Damn, I wish today had been the first time I ever met him."

"You mean you wish you hadn't turned from a rabbit to a chicken at Quimby's party," Diane retorted. "Everyone had a good laugh at the unmasking. I don't know why you had to turn it into a life-and-death situation. Just maybe, you could have had more than laughs with the Bandit."

"That's just the point, I was having more than laughs," Virginia snapped sarcastically. "Why do you think I ran?" She rubbed a heavy hand over her weary features. "I should have taken off the mask; running only made things worse. At that party and on that balcony I forgot who I really was and became totally absorbed in a fantasy."

"So?" Diane replied with a shrug. "Everyone's entitled to a little—"

"No, Diane." Virginia cut her off with a vehement shake of her head. "I'm not *everyone,* and I'm certainly not willing to play with explosives just for the sheer thrill of it. My career, my professional standing is the most important thing in my life—it *is* my life. I wouldn't jeopardize it for anything. Things are beginning to get easier for the professional woman now, but the last ten years have been hell for me. I've had my age, my brains, and my sex held against me. I've been able to overcome the odds, break through the discrimination barriers, and become a respected member of the scientific community. I'm conceited enough not to allow myself to be a source of amusement and ridicule for anyone." Virginia took a deep breath and straightened from the wall. "The only way out is to have Briarcliff send a replacement."

"No!" The word echoed in hollow tones. Diane hastily lowered her voice. "Dammit, Ginger, you can't do that!" She slapped her small, multiringed hand over Virginia's moving lips and jabbed a mauve-tinted fingernail against her chest. "You are letting your imagination run wild again. Alex Braddock doesn't suspect a thing. Why jump the gun? Now, I realize I had great expectations of your . . . well, your physical and mental makeover, but I will allow you to be the dull, boring physicist here at AVELCOMP."

Virginia lifted the constricting palm. "Gee, thanks, you're all heart."

"I'm only thinking of you," Diane told her in a sincere voice that matched her earnest expression. The effect was suddenly spoiled by a burst of giggles. "Just listen to you! You're beginning to talk like a human instead of a computer, you're looking better and . . . and don't try to deny you didn't have a little fun at the party or during our shopping spree."

Virginia rolled her eyes toward the ceiling but couldn't contain the smile that transformed the severity of her features. "I will admit that being with you has certainly relaxed my workaholic drives."

Diane lowered her mascara-coated lashes, her index finger rolling a tiny lint ball from the sleeve of her black and red chevron-striped sweater. "Thank you for that lovely compliment." She looked up at Virginia, her eyes wide and serious. "Listen, I have no doubts that you have paid your dues; in fact, I think you've probably paid a lot of other women's dues. But now is the time when you should reap the rewards of a decade of work, talent, and fame. There is no danger for you here."

Her pert features became animated by a wide grin. "Just to ease your mind, I'm going to check Mr. Braddock's reaction myself. I've got to get his signature on some company insurance forms." Diane's high heels tapped a steady beat against the gray floor tiles as they strode down the hallway to the personnel office. "Do you think he'll be in the lab?"

"Well, our lunch did run a bit longer than usual," Virginia looked pointedly at the wall clock.

"Those designer jeans were on sale," Diane retorted in quick defense. "They were a bargain."

The ultraviolet light in the air lock turned Virginia's oxford cloth shirt superwhite while the vibrating floor beneath her shoes shook infinitesimal dust particles from her clothing.

"This won't make me sterile, will it?" Diane asked, the oscillating pad making her voice quiver. She hugged the file folder to her breast while her eyes nervously surveyed the awesome, blue-violet-tinged chamber.

Virginia choked back a laugh. "It will cleanse your body of harmful bacteria," she intoned with affected professional solemnity. When the buzzer sounded, she pushed open the laboratory door. The fluorescent lights were on, but the only visible occupants were six large equipment crates, with SoLAs stenciled on the wooden frames, which had been left in the center of the room.

Diane winked and fluffed out her blond waves. "Mr. Braddock?" There was no response. "Men always take longer lunches than women; they just never admit it. I'll wait a few minutes." She dropped into a bleached oak side chair, fumbled in the pocket of her black pleated skirt for a cigarette, then wrinkled her nose at the prominent red-lettered NO SMOKING sign.

Virginia looked up from inspecting the lading bills taped to a six-foot crate. "This looks interesting, but I've got a report to type and—" her final words became mangled in her throat, while her tan leather clutch fell from numb fingers and slapped the linoleum.

"What's the matter? What is it? Is it a bug!" Diane lunged to her feet, the file papers scattering in her wake.

"On . . . on the desk . . ." Virginia pointed with a shaky finger, then clamped a hand over her mouth, her stomach reeling in shock.

"Oh, my God!"

Four ever widening blue eyes stared in petrified terror at the fluffy, white bunny tail positioned dead center on Virginia's green desk blotter.

"He knew . . . he knows . . . he . . ."

"Take it easy." Diane grabbed Virginia's sleeve, the broadcloth tightly clutched inside a white knuckled fist.

"Take it easy?" She tore her eyes from the desk and gaped in open-mouthed amazement at her friend. "The only thing I'm going to take is the first plane back to Florida!" Virginia yanked her arm free. Her breathing came fast and shallow; she was hyperventilating. "I knew it wasn't my imagination. I won't be able to look that man in the eye, let alone work with him. My credibility and my integrity aren't worth the fuzz on that tail!"

"Will you please shut up so I can think!" Diane hissed, pushing her against the packing crate.

"Oh no! I'm going to do my own thinking." Virginia's nostrils flared in anger. "I've had enough of your logic." She moved Diane aside with Amazonian ease. "One phone call will do it. I will not—"

The air-lock door swung open to admit Alex Braddock. He was totally engrossed with a schematic until the square toe of his black leather boot collided with Virginia's purse. The clutch spiraled across the floor, further scattering the spilled insurance papers.

Alex studied the curious litter for a moment, then raised his smoky gaze to focus on two women, frozen in a tug-of-war position with the telephone receiver. A triangle of eyes formed, locked onto one another, then jointly lowered to stare at the furry desktop ornament.

"It seems every time I come in here that poor telephone is the recipient of some sort of violence." Alex tossed the rolled blueprint on a crate before rescuing Pacific Bell's equipment from twenty suddenly lax fingers. Plucking the white tail from the blotter, he favored their distraught feminine faces with an easy grin and began to juggle the fuzzy ball between two large capable hands.

Virginia and Diane followed the airborne acrobatics with nervous, shifting eyes; their foreheads and upper lips were beaded with perspiration, belying the climate-controlled atmosphere. A decidedly amused masculine voice made them look at each other in breath-holding consternation.

"I've spent the entire day going from office to office," Alex drawled, the humorous glint in his eyes echoed by the tone in his voice, "rather like Prince Charming, seeking not what foot fits the slipper but what derriere fits this tail."

He stood in front of Virginia's rigid form and positioned the furry ball boutonnierelike on her shirt.

"Actually it took very little deductive reasoning on my part." Alex's voice was low and vibrant and smooth as treacle. "You're the perfect height." His hands silhouetted her torso and defined the curve of her waist. He pressed her stiff figure against his hard body. "I remember how perfectly the vital parts met."

The toes on her shoes butted against his boots,

their knees touched, and Virginia could feel the sinewy strength in his thighs flex against her own. Two belt buckles clicked a metallic, musical note; her soft full breasts became squashed against his jacket.

There was only a marginal difference in their height at the shoulders, but Virginia felt she was dealing with a towering monolith—one whose lips, nose, and hypnotic agate eyes were scant inches from her own.

Her outward appearance remained calm, cool, and composed, but her traitorous mind replayed those Halloween memories: her thoughts kept taunting; her body started reacting. The touch of his hands, the scent of his skin, the warmth of his eyes ignited a purely physical, purely female, purely erotic spark.

Her breasts swelled, the nipples forming hard buds that dented the striped shirting. The very essence of her femininity was aroused by a heated rush. It was a total body experience.

"That perfume you wear left a haunting legacy that tantalized my mind all weekend," Alex murmured, his breath vibrating against her ear. "Then there're your eyes. No one else possesses those iridescent shards that harbor rainbows. I've retasted the sweetness of your lips hundreds of times, and my ears rang with the memory of your voice."

He took a step backward. His hands left her waist to slide through her hair, lifting the thick waves like a fan, luxuriating in the soft brown curls that hugged and caressed his fingers. "This . . . now this seems different. I remember it was laced with molten gold . . . or was it the reflection of the moon and the stars?"

Alex walked behind her. His face was still close to hers as his knuckles slithered down the supple length of her spine. "But no one in this building has such a memorable anatomy." His palm curved with familiarity over the rounded contours of her buttocks. "Unless there are two of you, I think I've found my disappearing Rabbit."

Diane viewed Virginia's paralyzed body and pale, traumatized features with total empathy. She'd seen that same expression in Bambi's mother's eyes in that memorable Disney animation.

Well, she wasn't going to let Virginia die. Her hand automatically curled around the cellophane package in her skirt pocket. A cigarette always made thinking easier and more profound. Unfortunately she didn't have the time for that luxury. Action was needed—needed now!

The situation needed a savior. Someone bold, someone daring, someone provocative—an idea clicked. Why not use that same *someone* who instigated this mess? Why not resurrect *Ginger*!

Diane inhaled a deep lungful of air, imagined it was tobacco, exhaled it slowly, then led the battle charge. "I'm afraid, Mr. Braddock, you have stumbled onto our . . . our little secret." She sounded nauseatingly contrite. "I hope you won't tell. You know how upset Mr. Quimby would be if he finds out

I brought a substitute to his party instead of Dr. Farrell."

For the first time Alex remembered there was a third person in the lab. He gave his head a sharp shake, and his gaze reluctantly left Virginia's slim throat to focus on Diane's innocent blue eyes and apologetic half-smile. "I . . . I beg your pardon?"

Diane settled herself comfortably on the corner of the desk, taking the time to arrange both the pleats on her skirt and her strategy.

She already felt enormously pleased at the shift in Alex's attention, fancying herself the sailor who had successfully tacked her ship. Now it was ploy, gambit, ploy. "I think we can trust and confide in Mr. Braddock, don't you, Doctor?"

Virginia's eyes widened, and she nodded dumbly.

Diane favored Alex with her most disarming smile. "You know the three of us were like . . . like triplets back in Idaho."

"Three of you?" Alex raised a skeptical dark brow, crossed his arms, and leaned back against a tall crate.

She nodded and let her gaze wander from his quizzical expression to Virginia's amazed features. "What can I tell you about two sisters who are as different as . . . lumpy oatmeal and lemon soufflé?" Diane's mouth formed a petite moue. Her chest rose beneath a heavy sigh. "Virginia here was the studious one. Staggering IQ, astounding grades, teacher's pet, wet blanket, antisocial, totally nonorgasmic." She blithely ignored the malevolent daggers thrown in her direction.

"Ginger was just the opposite, despite the fact that they are twins. She was always in trouble at school, the IQ of a houseplant—getting a D was a major accomplishment. Why, she even has trouble reading a digital watch! But Ginger is very popular. She gets turned on by the navel in an orange!"

Diane's red glossed lips curved into a reminiscent smile. "I had the best of both worlds living next door to the Farrell twins. Virginia kept me sensible and did my homework while Ginger added spice and excitement to my life."

Alex massaged his jaw with due consideration. "Are you telling me that the woman I met at Quimby's was Dr. Farrell's twin?" he asked, his eyes narrowing in doubt.

"It was all my idea." Diane nodded. "Ginger flew in for a modeling assignment, and when I couldn't persuade the doctor to attend the party, her sister was only too happy to substitute. I didn't think anyone would notice. But that Ginger . . ." She rolled her eyes, her tongue clicking against the roof of her mouth. "She never plays it cool or safe. She has to get involved, has to get intense, loves to play games." She gave a futile shrug.

Deciding not to wait for Alex's rebuttal, Diane plunged ahead with vigor. "You know, Mr. Braddock, if you saw them side by side you would realize just how different they really are." She favored Virginia with a purposeful stare, hoping she would abandon her mute, robotlike position and begin to cooperate and contribute.

"That's very true, when we are together the differences are quite pronounced." The strength in her voice made Virginia feel more secure. She decided to further pursue her advantage.

Virginia drew herself up to regal proportions, at the same time managing to cave her chest in. "My sister is much shorter than I am. Of course, you remember her height with heels." Her hands flattened her tumbled hair and looped it behind her ears, making her face resemble a square, stern block.

"Ginger is a blonde. It's all artificial, but then, models rely on cosmetics to create various effects in their appearance." The pomposity of her tone harmonized with her disdainful manner. "My sister's eyes are more gray than blue and, since her arrival, everything reeks of that cloying perfume she uses."

Diane exhaled a prisoned breath and slid off the desk. "When we came in and found the rabbit's tail, well . . . you can imagine how upset we were." She favored Alex with a wide stare. "Ginger told us about her escapade with the Bandit, but we never thought we'd be the ones dealing with him." Diane viewed the mottled red flush that stained his features with well-concealed jubilation.

"Yes," Virginia inserted in a quick, brusque tone, "I really must apologize for my sister. I should be used to her antics and tidying up after her, but I still find these situations quite abhorrent."

"I think I'm the one owing the apologies." Alex slid a long finger between tie and collar, hoping to ease the discomfort. "The more I look at you, Dr.

Farrell, the more I realize just how mistaken I am. It's very apparent that the frivolity of a masquerade party is well beneath your dignified station."

"Correct," Virginia agreed haughtily. "My work is the only source of enrichment I need in my life." Why did that statement suddenly become the biggest lie told yet? Swallowing the sour taste that had formed in her mouth, Virginia continued with brutal determination. "My sister is the type who thrives on diversions, whereas I thrive on constants."

"Your strengths are both commendable and admirable, Doctor." Alex's smooth Southern drawl was once again full of compliments. "I will, of course, keep your little deception a secret."

Diane grabbed his hand and pumped it in false gratitude. "Thank you, Mr. Braddock. You don't know how relieved I am. I've worked at AVELCOMP for three years and would hate to lose face with Mr. Quimby."

Alex could do nothing but consolingly pat the small ringed hand that held his in a Herculean grip. He found his eyes had once again focused on Virginia; his mind, however, remembered Ginger. "Dr. Farrell, I was wondering when your sister would be avail—" The telephone's insistent buzz interrupted him.

Saved by Bell. Virginia breathed and scooped up the receiver. She listened for a minute, gave a mental sigh, and hung up. "That was the receiving dock, Mr. Braddock. Another equipment truck just arrived, and they would like you to come down and assist in the setup."

"I'll head right over." Alex nodded, reaching for the rolled schematic on the packing crate. "I was wondering though when and where I could reach Ging—"

"Mr. Braddock," Diane's sweet, melodic voice interrupted him, "would you please scrawl your name on these insurance forms. I have to process them today." She pushed the rescued, now neatly packaged papers under his nose, flipped the pages, and pointed to the appropriate dotted lines.

When Alex had signed in five places, Diane neatly juggled the folder under her arm and escorted him to the door. "You really are a pet." She smiled up at him. "I'm sure you'll enjoy working with us at AVELCOMP, but one important rule here is never keep the boys in shipping and receiving waiting." She unlatched the metal portal and deftly shoved Alex into the air lock.

Diane collapsed against the closed doorway, shut her eyes, and exhaled a musical breath. "That was a stroke of genius, if I do say so myself." Her lashes fluttered open, her lips curling into a cocky grin. "Now, don't thank me, it—"

"Thank you! I was thinking more of murder!" With narrowed eyes and intent, purposeful strides, Virginia advanced on her.

"Wait just one minute!" Diane scooted behind a low, wide crate, anxious to separate intended victim from assailant. "I'm the one who just saved that '*memorable anatomy*' of yours."

"Saved it?" The words split on a high note of hysteria. Virginia's clenched fist hit the crate, nearly splintering a wooden slat. "It seems to me you've thrown it right into a raging inferno. Whatever possessed you to make up such a story? How could you have created another person? I may have been guilty of some big lies in my time, but this . . . this . . . this . . ." Words evaded her; her head collapsed into her hands.

"I don't know why you're so upset." Diane sniffed in an injured voice. "I was only trying to help. I remembered all the times your lies saved me."

Virginia looked up, opened one eye, and focused it on her slump-shouldered friend like a malevolent cyclops. "We are not teenagers, and this is not high school," she growled, then became more demonstrative. "Lest you forget, Diane, we are nearly thirty, much too old to play such games."

"Men and women have been playing games since the dawn of time; you just haven't participated," she countered with haughty self-righteousness. Then, as if to salve her conscience, she added, "It wasn't actually a lie—we just economized the truth. You were another person at the party and on that balcony."

"That was one night, after too many drinks," Virginia grated, her lips thinning in anger. "You're trying to perpetuate a myth. You're trying to mix fantasy and reality. That only works in romances. This is real life!"

Diane favored her with a blithe smile and seemed totally ignorant of the narrowed, intimidating glare cast in her direction. "It also seems that you, as Ginger, made quite a memorable impression on Alex Braddock."

Virginia opened her mouth, then closed it, unable to think of a suitable retort.

"You obviously fascinated the man. Doesn't that tell you something about yourself?" Diane's petite features turned serious. She grasped Virginia's cold hands and gave them supportive warmth. "With just a little initiative you can grab the gusto that is life. Aren't you tired of sitting on the sidelines? Your job may be mentally and professionally rewarding, but what about . . . sensually? Believe me, an encounter with a flesh and blood man beats a clunking, metallic robot any day!"

"What do you want from me?" The words were uttered from deep within a lacerated, exhausted soul.

"I want you to take an interest in yourself for a change; to stop being so insecure and appreciate what you've accomplished. You have so much to offer. What makes you think you can't attract and hold a man just because you've got brains and talent and a high-powered career?"

"Because it's happened before."

"So what? Do you think that makes it carved in granite?" Diane snorted derisively. "He was the insecure one. Why did you accept the blame? And worse, why have you let it fester and infect your life?"

"It's easier to blunt the senses than to keep getting

hurt," Virginia explained in a weary voice. "My professional responsibilities complicate my personal life."

Diane released her hold and looked at her friend's lowered head for a long moment. A myriad of thoughts tumbled through her mind; she took a deep breath and plunged ahead. "Are you attracted to Alex?"

"Yes."

"Would you like Alex to be attracted to you?"

"Yes."

"Well then?"

Virginia looked at her. "He wants Ginger."

"You are Ginger!"

"No, I'm not!"

"But you could be," Diane prodded resolutely. "You were Ginger once, and you were terrific."

Running her fingers through her tumbled hair, Virginia let her palms ease the tension from the nape of her neck. "I refuse to resort to any more trickery," she returned with equally stubborn determination.

"All's fair in love and war."

"I am not in love!" she squealed through clenched teeth.

"But you do find Alex attractive," Diane pointed out tenaciously. "Physically attractive, mentally attractive, and sexually attractive."

"Yes, yes, yes, yes!" Virginia exploded. "But that's not love. It's . . . it's more like spontaneous combustion." Her last words were mumbled.

"Well," Diane continued in a sly vein, "at least

you admit the man causes a definite chemical reaction. That's quite an accomplishment." She cast her a glance. "Now that Alex believes there are two of you, you'll be able to stay and work in the lab and not worry about losing his respect."

"I suppose so," Virginia nodded in slow agreement.

"Although I don't know how you're going to do it." Diane tapped the folder of insurance forms against her hip, then sauntered toward the air lock. "It's going to take a lot of willpower to ignore the sensations Alex can cause. Those broad shoulders, that sensuous mouth, those bedroom eyes—it's going to be pure torture, especially when you remember the balcony."

Diane circled her ruby-glossed lips slowly with her tongue, then exhaled a dramatic sigh worthy of an Oscar. "Shoulder to shoulder, thigh to thigh. Day in, day out. Look, but don't touch. So near, yet so far. I could never do it. I'd have Alex Braddock out of his clothes, on the floor, and in a state of rapture in no time."

She smiled into Virginia's distressed features. "But I keep forgetting what a Rock of Gibraltar you are. Ginger's the one with the warm, passionate, sensual nature; you're the unfeeling, frigid fish."

A pair of brooding blue eyes stared at the slowly closing door. For the rest of the afternoon, Diane's erotic words, coupled by visions of Alex, tormented Virginia's resolve.

* * *

"Am I still invited for dinner?"

Virginia plucked the wine bottle from the ringed hand beneath her nose, then looked down into Diane's pensive face. "Of course." She stepped to one side, bowed, and made a grand, sweeping gesture with her other hand. "I'm sure you'll find tonight's menu most appropriate for this hostess." Her features were totally unreadable. "I'm serving a relative—baked fish."

Diane choked, cleared her throat, and flounced past her toward the dining room. "All right, I admit my parting comment was quite uncalled for. I'm sorry."

"That's all right." Virginia's mouth twisted into a wry smile. "I've been thinking about some of your comments all afternoon."

"And?"

"I'm still thinking," came her dry rejoinder just before she disappeared through the archway into the kitchen.

Diane made a face, extracted cigarettes, lighter, and an ashtray from the pocket of her batik-print jump suit before settling herself at the table. "Did Alex ever come back to the lab?"

"No."

She made another face, then sucked in a soothing lungful of smoke. "Dinner smells great. I didn't think you had it in you, Julia Child."

"I don't." Virginia reappeared, her pot holdered hands bearing two obvious TV dinners. "I let those scientists, chemists, and nutritionists in the frozen-food industry be creative for me." She placed an aluminum-foil-covered tray on each flowered place mat.

"What about the antipasto?" Diane looked inquiringly at the individual wooden salad bowls filled with colorful vegetables glistening with oil, vinegar, and herb dressing.

"The Italian deli on the corner," she returned matter-of-factly, shaking her hands free from the oven mitts. Virginia reached for the bottle of rosé and intently studied the label with the vengeance of a connoisseur. "Napa Valley. A week ago Thursday. Perfect!" She twisted off the cap and poured.

Laughter erupted from both women, filling the room with joyous camaraderie. Stubbing out her cigarette, Diane grinned up at Virginia. "I don't know why I expected anything different. As I recall, you got suspended from home ec for setting fires in the ovens."

"That was the only thing I never did deliberately." Virginia's mouth twisted into a rueful smile. "I really missed not having a mother to teach me to cook and sew. I hoped home ec would do the job, but somehow I don't think it would have helped. I easily accomplish the most difficult scientific problems, but cooking, baking, and general housekeeping elude me." Her blue eyes rolled toward the ceiling. "Thank heaven for housekeepers, laundry services, and processed foods. For me the best cookbook is the yellow pages, and the handiest kitchen appliance is the telephone."

The laughter faded from Diane's face. She picked up the crystal wineglass and stared somberly into the shimmering pink liquid. "It must have been rough on you. When you have parents and a family you tend to take them for granted. Sometimes you even think you'd be better off without all their nagging and interference. But when you don't have them . . ." Her voice trailed off.

"When you don't have them, you learn to compensate," Virginia finished in an even tone. "It does color your attitude on life. Little stains that are embedded forever. It changes the way you think, the way you feel, the way you relate."

She cleared her throat and pushed the memories from her mind. "I made a promise to myself that we were not going to be serious tonight." Virginia smiled at her friend. "You want me to be lively and bright and witty, so you are the one I'm going to practice on."

Diane lifted her glass in silent approval. She studied Virginia's appearance with critical delight. Long brown hair had been pulled into an off-center topknot anchored by two cloisonné chopsticks; her face was still flushed from the heat of the oven, and the mannish work clothes had been discarded, replaced by a navy silk kabuki robe etched with a screen of cherry blossoms.

"You look very"—Diane had been about to say "Gingerish" but thought better of it—"exotic."

Tucking her hands inside the wide kimono sleeves, Virginia gave an oriental-inspired bow. "I think I told you that I spent last year working with a toy company, but I failed to mention it was in Japan." She settled in the opposite chair.

"I fell in love with Tokyo. The people are courteous, respectful, and full of tradition. The laboratory was housed in a graceful temple surrounded by breathtaking gardens. There was a lot of work to be done, but somehow the tranquil environment lessened the stress."

"My big travel adventure has been from Boise to here." Diane grinned as she tore open the aluminum covering on her dinner. "One of these days I'll travel to some faraway land, take a cruise, maybe hike across Europe . . . one of these days."

She grimaced at the food on the metal plate. "The least you could have done was learned to cook Japanese," she mumbled and reached for more wine.

"Give it a chance," Virginia coaxed, cutting into the steaming buttered flounder with paprika and stuffed with crabmeat. "You only get dessert if you clean your plate. And I've defrosted everybody's favorite, Sara Lee cheesecake."

"The one with strawberries?" At her affirmative nod Diane emitted a low groan. "That's bribery! Do you know I once ate one still frozen?" She took a deep breath, then proceeded to attack her dinner. Her eyebrows arched in pleasant surprise. The entrée proved almost gourmet; the peas and tiny pearl onions were tender yet crisp; even the whipped potatoes were not as gluey as she expected.

Dinner and dessert were garnished with heavy

doses of laughter and girlish giggles, travel stories and love tales retold, details embellished courtesy of the rapidly emptying bottle of rosé.

"Do you want any coffee?" Virginia asked, her forehead puckering at the difficulty she had in forming those few words.

Diane shook her head. "I don't want to sober the glow." She smiled and reached for a cigarette. "You really are quite the conversationalist. Your trips are fascinating, and so is your work."

"Thank you." Virginia felt a rush of heat surging to her face, and she wriggled uncomfortably on the chair cushion. "I haven't talked so much in ages," she confessed, then whispered: "I think it's the wine."

"I think you're just relaxed and confident about your subject," Diane told her with inebriated wisdom.

Elbows on the table, her flushed cheeks balanced on the palms of her hands, Virginia looked inquiringly. "Do you really think I'm interesting? I'm usually content to sit and listen unless someone asks specifics." All the *s*'s got tangled in her teeth, her thickened tongue clearing them away.

"You are very interesting; you are very knowledgeable; and you are very attractive." Diane waved her hands to emphasize each point, then began slapping out the burning ashes that scattered across the antique pink tabletop. "What do you think I've been trying to tell you!" Her voice became shrill but not from anger.

"It would be wonderful if Alex Braddock thought so," Virginia mumbled on a wistful note, her full mouth pouting childishly. "I'd give anything if he would—" The ringing telephone startled her; her face slipped from the hands that cradled it. With slow, fumbling movements Virginia leaned her chair backward toward the serving counter and scooped up the receiver. "Dr. Farrell." The words were delivered in rote.

"Good evening, Doctor. This is Alex Braddock."

She didn't need to hear the confirmation of his name. The deep baritone that rolled through the line like smooth, aged bourbon caressed her ear and evoked instant visualization.

Virginia made a grab for the table edge to keep herself and the chair from crashing to the carpet. "H-e-l-l-o, A-l-e-x." Each letter stuttered to life. She took a deep breath, made a valiant effort to remain calm, and hoped the fog that shrouded her brain would lift faster than the smog that covered L.A.

Diane was by her side in an instant. Now there were two ears, two alcohol-dulled brains, and two pounding hearts waiting in anticipatory panic.

"I missed seeing you this afternoon," his charming voice soothed. "I just wanted to let you know the lab is no longer a cluttered mess, and Glendale sent a robot for you to work on."

Virginia began to breathe at her normal rate. "That was very thoughtful of you." Diane rolled her eyes, then pantomimed wildly for her to be less formal. "I don't usually leave so early," she continued, feeling more relaxed, a definite lilt in her voice, "but I had a few outside errands to run." She leaned back in the chair, gaining more confidence every minute; Diane patted her hand encouragingly.

"I'm just so very glad that we got the Halloween mix-up straightened out today," came his casual remark. "I do hope you won't hold it against me."

"Of course not," Virginia gave a carefree laugh. "I am looking forward to working with you and learning more about lasers and solar energy. I think we will make an exciting team." She looked at Diane, who nodded vigorously.

"I'm sure we will, Doctor. . . ." Alex paused, then cleared his throat. "I'd like to speak with Ginger for a moment, if I might."

"G . . . G . . . Ginger?" The Sara Lee began to burn its way back up her digestive tract. Virginia closed her eyes; beads of perspiration glistened on her forehead.

"Yes," he persisted. "You did say she was staying with you."

Virginia looked at Diane, mouthed "did we," and received a confused shrug in response. Diane quickly grabbed a pencil from the counter and a white paper napkin.

Squinting at the scribbled, practically illegible words, Virginia read aloud, "Ginger flew to Tokyo on a modeling assignment and will be back early Friday." Horrified, she pointed to the word *Friday*.

"Tokyo!" Alex echoed in surprise.

"Well," she tried vainly to keep things light, but

her words sounded brittle, "my sister is a great one for fluttering from one place to another for her job." Virginia swallowed the uncomfortable lump of lies wedged in her throat. "Ginger will be sorry she missed you."

"She won't have a thing to be sorry about," Alex returned in a brusque, autocratic tone. "Tell Ginger that I will pick her up at eight on Friday, and I won't take *any* excuse—short of a plane crash. See you tomorrow, Doctor."

Diane replaced the receiver. "Plane crash"—her lips twisted—"how gory!" She dropped into a chair and lit her last cigarette.

"How could you?" Virginia breathed angrily at her. "Friday! Now what are we going to do?"

"Relax," she countered evenly. "We've got four days to think of something—unless you decide to go out with him." Diane flashed her a hopeful glance.

"I was thinking more in terms of hara-kiri," Virginia muttered and rested her chin on the table. "A few minutes ago I was praying the man would call."

"He did."

"But it wasn't me he asked for."

"You could go after him. You could fight for him," Diane pointed out. "Try turning on the charm during the day and maybe the next time he'll ask for Virginia."

Two blue eyes stared at her for a long uncomfortable moment before they disappeared behind weary lids.

CHAPTER FIVE

With her lips stained fuchsia from consuming half a bottle of Pepto-Bismol, her blue eyes dulled from lack of sleep, and her nerves splintered by anxiety, Virginia gamely subjected herself to the exorcising rituals inside the air lock.

Last night Diane's final parting pearl of wisdom had been "Every woman should have a secret—it gives her an air of mystery." Well, Virginia grimaced, she had one hell of a secret, and all it had given her was a nervous stomach and insomnia!

She had spent the entire night twittering about the apartment like a tremulous caged parakeet, carrying on one-sided gibberish conversations with herself and drinking countless cups of warm milk.

She had tried lying in bed, listening to soothing music and hoping it would transport her into the arms of Morpheus. But the drifting, darting shadows that played along the ceiling seemed choreographed to the haunting strains of trumpet and saxophone. They proved to be a mental stimulant, provoking memories of dancing on the balcony in Alex's arms.

With little effort the swirling, orchestrated shadows became three-dimensional man-and-woman images. Virginia became the voyeur, watching Alex and her other self recreate the romance of Halloween night.

Sights, sounds, and her heightened senses made the memories more vivid, more real. Her ears vibrated against the languid deep-voiced echo that was Alex's. Her nose dismissed the scent of freshly washed linen, replacing it with a crisp, assertive male cologne. Her lips clung to an imaginary masculine mouth while her body tingled against the remembered muscular strength of him. She had wanted to capture time in a bottle and, ironically, it seemed she had. An erotic souvenir, devil-bent on haunting her.

Angry, Virginia had dragged herself free from this carnal bondage and had taken refuge in the stark, fluorescent-lit kitchen. There she spent the remaining lonely hours cleaning the inside of a nearly empty refrigerator and neatening drawers of untouched cooking utensils.

But that inner devil successfully tempted those diligent hands to become idle while it provoked her mind to become reactive. If she wanted to again capture the magic and passion of being with Alex, she had only to become Ginger on Friday night. Would it be so wrong? Who would get hurt?

Not Alex—he would reap the rewards. Not Ginger—she would be free to seduce and partake. But what about Virginia? Her sensible, lucid self would be caged and banished for the night, consumed by a sensual flirting soul that had escaped from an intellectual prison.

While Virginia had never believed much in astrology, she knew her birthdate placed her in the third house of the zodiac—Gemini. It was symbolized by twin constellations and two-sided personalities—talk about typecasting!

But was it really possible for one body to house two such opposite entities and not be committed to an asylum? Virginia wondered if other women suffered from this curse. She had few women friends. None, save Diane, that she had ever confided in, and she was just now realizing how much she missed that type of relationship.

She had worked hard in her chosen field to overcome a variety of discriminatory barriers. While never in doubt about her professional abilities, Virginia often wondered about her abilities as a woman. Her personal relationships, granted there had been few, had soured rapidly. Working so many years in cryogenics and robotics had turned her into a frozen automaton, devoid of feelings.

Was that really necessary anymore? She was well respected in her profession. Maybe Diane was right. Now was the time to loosen up and enjoy life. Integrate Ginger's joie de vivre into Virginia's sobriety. It was the toughest problem she'd ever faced.

The green all-clear signal flashed on. Virginia wiped her hands, which were damp with perspiration, on pleated olive twill trousers, took a deep breath, pasted a sickly smile on her face, and let her khaki leather sport shoes drag her reluctant anatomy into the lab.

"Good morning, Doctor." Alex looked up, a testing probe in his hand, and flashed her a brief smile.

Virginia swallowed and managed to speak past the uncomfortable lump in her throat to parrot his greeting. As she slid a lab coat over her desert-toned checked shirt she found her gaze had drifted back to study her work-engrossed colleague.

Alex looked different this morning. Gone was the formal three-piece business suit he'd worn on their initial meeting. In its place were casual work clothes: well-cut boot-length denims and a close-fitting cream and navy pullover. He was more approachable. More like the Bandit. Sleek, powerful, and full of animal energy.

Suddenly Virginia felt an all-consuming need to approach him. Tucking a few stray wisps of hair into her sleek yet feminine chignon, she moved closer to his work table. "Well, you certainly didn't exaggerate when you said the lab was back to normal." She looked with approval at the neat equipment racks lining the previously unoccupied south wall. "You must have been here half the night."

Alex switched off the probe, scribbled a few notations on his clipboard pad, then tossed his pencil aside. "I could sense how important order was to you, Doctor."

She turned her face away and winced. Yesterday's impression was not the same as the one made Halloween night. Virginia moistened her lips and put a lilt in her voice. "You'll be surprised to learn that when I work I'm rather like Hansel and Gretel, leaving a trail of instruments and crumbled notes behind me."

"Now, I find that very difficult to believe." He shook his head, a lock of silver-etched dark hair falling across his forehead. "I picture your work habits like a well-orchestrated assembly line—neat, clean, and precise."

Virginia yanked a pen from her breast pocket and clicked it furiously. Being compared to mechanized automation was getting on her nerves! "Well, that just shows you how wrong first impressions can be," came her childish retort.

Alex stood in front of her, his smoke-colored eyes level with her iridescent blue ones. "I'm a great believer in first impressions," came his languid rejoiner. "Now, your sister . . . well, Ginger I can visualize as being"—Alex's eyes grew brighter, his lips curving into a reminiscent smile—"enchantingly disorganized."

Virginia's features turned to granite. "You mean slovenly."

"Enticingly tousled," he continued, his Southern drawl growing more pronounced.

"Messy and unkempt," she grated through clenched teeth.

"Sensual and alluring."

"Cheap and brazen!"

"My goodness." Alex's brow arched in surprise.

"I had no idea there was such a rivalry between the two of you."

"Rivalry! There's no rivalry!" Virginia all but exploded, the ballpoint pen stabbing the air near his chest. "I just know Ginger for what she really is. Your memories are colored by moonlight, music, and martinis!"

He rescued the pen from her white-knuckled hand. "You might be right." Alex's face turned serious. His gaze darkened and locked onto hers. "But then I'll discover how right or wrong I am on Friday night." His long, capable fingers slid the ballpoint down her shoulder into her breast pocket.

"By the way," he adroitly turned the conversation back to business, "your robot is over there with a twenty-page trouble ticket. I'm working on the solar battery for him right now."

Virginia took a deep, steadying breath, tried to ignore the tingling sensation in her left breast, and moved past him to tackle a less physically and mentally disturbing problem.

"He's driving me crazy!" The plastic catsup container made a wheezing sound as Virginia viciously strangled its middle. "All Alex talks about is Ginger, Ginger, Ginger! She's sooo wonderful!" Virginia mimicked in a catty, nasal tone.

Diane poured a neat dab of catsup on one corner of her cardboard container, picked up a crisp, golden french fry, and elegantly dipped it into the condiment.

"You know," Virginia continued roughly, throwing open her hamburger bun, "men are the most fickle, easily dazzled creatures on God's green earth." She removed two pickles, squirted on more catsup, then smashed the bun back together. "All Alex remembers is some blond sex goddess by moonlight. He's not interested in a real woman—just a lustful fantasy."

Diane took a dainty bite of her chicken sandwich and shrugged in silent consideration.

"It would serve that man right if Ginger did go out with him tomorrow," Virginia mumbled through a mouthful of beef, tomatoes, cheese, and onions. She swallowed, her eyes narrowing menacingly. "I don't think Alex could tolerate an evening of breathless gasps, cutesy, illiterate trivia, and a body propelled by nonstop hormones."

Diane nodded mutely, wiped her mouth on a napkin emblazoned with golden arches, and took a sip of black coffee.

"Three hours *tops,* and Ginger would disgust him." Virginia stabbed the air with a catsup-laden french fry. "Alex is an intelligent, highly educated engineer. Why would he want to pursue a creature like Ginger? What could they possibly have in common? No, no, I'm sure he'd be bored to tears."

Diane merely shrugged and nodded again, picking up the salt shaker to reenhance the french fries.

"I've been working with Alex for three days now, and I know a lot more about him than I did last weekend," Virginia explained on a much calmer note. "He is brilliant in his work. I've watched him agonize over minor details, exhaust himself on alternatives, and casually dismiss his successes."

Her lips curved into a soft smile, her blue eyes glittering in the colors of a prism. "He asks my opinion and takes my suggestions. And, Diane, he gets more excited about my accomplishments than I do." Virginia could almost feel Alex's hand on her shoulders, giving her a complimentary squeeze.

She exhaled a rather dreamy sigh and propped her glowing cheeks in her hands. "We've been taking our coffee breaks together in the lounge. I know all about the projects he's worked on, his life in New Orleans, his apartment, and his family. His parents sound wonderful, and he's got three sisters and two brothers and a slew of nieces and nephews."

Her hand hit the small wooden restaurant table, sending a shower of cola and coffee over the assorted disposable dinnerware. "That's why I don't understand his preoccupation with—Ginger." She spat the word out with extreme distaste. "Every time we work together Alex has to bring her name into the conversation.

"She's charming, she's sensuous, she's alluring, she's adorable," Virginia mimicked, then grew angry. "I'm sturdy, industrious, sensible, inventive, and dependable. I sound like a pair of orthopedic shoes!

"To me Alex is more than the Bandit on the balcony. He has depth, feelings, and meaning," she said in a rough tone. "And yet all he thinks about is that harebrain, Ginger. What's the matter with him?

You'd think a man like that would want substance rather than fluff." Virginia's fist slapped the table again. "I'm willing to bet that an evening of whipped cream will have him craving potatoes."

Diane calmly collected the garbage and arranged it in neat order on the plastic tray. "Since you're already stocked with potatoes, I think we better go shopping for the whipped cream."

"Huh? Virginia blinked at her in dumb confusion.

"Ginger would never wear sensible tweeds and broadcloth. And while we have perked up your wardrobe to some degree, there is nothing truly glamorous hanging in your closet." Diane rubbed her hands together with enthusiasm. "The stores are open late tonight. We'll find the most stunning, suggestive, enticing clothes in town. Tomorrow night you'll set Alex's pulse racing and make his wildest fantasies come true."

"I . . . I will?"

She nodded solemnly, stood up, and literally dragged Virginia from her chair. "Don't worry about a thing." Diane patted the cold, clammy hand trapped between hers. "I'll design the gun—all you have to do is pull the trigger."

Virginia sat on a pink boudoir stool in the center of a pink-and-orange-striped dressing room and stared into the wraparound mirrors. Hanging on assorted hooks was a collection of fashions that bared more than they covered and seeming to guarantee a most smoldering night. But the mousy, shy, uneasy woman who had spent two hours trying on creations of glitter and glamour suddenly knew she couldn't pull it off.

"The saleswoman is writing up the order," Diane said, poking her head through the opening in the orange curtain. "What's the matter?"

"Everything." Virginia pointed at her reflection and shook her head in disgust. "What about this?" Her hands clutched fistfuls of drab, lifeless hair that had snapped its rubber-banded bonds and tumbled haphazardly about her shoulders. "Ginger's a blonde. How can I be a brunette tomorrow morning and a blonde tomorrow night?"

"Well . . ." Diane's mouth twisted expressively. "I was going to suggest a wig . . . but with Alex's penchant for ruffling fingers through your hair—"

"He'd think he'd scalped me!" Virginia finished morosely. She closed her eyes and groaned. "It's not going to work. It's dumb and high schoolish. It just won't work." Her eyes flew open. "Why don't we kill her? A car crash on the way home from the airport?" She looked hopeful.

Diane shook her head. "He'd want to go to the funeral." She rubbed her chin for a thoughtful moment, then snapped her fingers. "I should have thought of this before. I'll call Joan."

"Joan?"

"Joan Enright—she's my neighbor. She works for the best hair salon in L.A.," Diane explained, her blue eyes regaining their former enthusiastic glow.

"You get dressed. I'll give her a call and explain our problem."

"I don't know, Di." Virginia's voice was muffled by the cinnamon sweat-shirt dress she was pulling over her head. "I felt more confident with a costume and mask."

"Your clothes will be your costume; makeup and hair will be your mask," Diane told her in a tone of patient forbearance. "You're the one who wants to show Alex that whipped cream, while tempting, is also sickening. One night should do it!"

"Then, why did we buy half a dozen outfits?" she countered with heavy sarcasm as she wrapped a leather sash around her slim waist.

Diane flashed her a lurid grin. "That's just in case *you* decide that you like being fluff instead of substance."

Virginia finished dressing while Diane ran off to call Joan. Examining the clothes hanging on the dressing room hooks, she slid them off and threw them over her arm. As she walked toward the cashier she saw Diane hurrying across the floor toward her. Excitement was brimming in her eyes. "It's all set. We'll go straight to Joan's from here."

Virginia wriggled in self-conscious discomfort beneath the flowing plastic cape and eyed her two companions. They discussed her as if she weren't even there.

Diane, her petite figure cocooned in a pale-blue jogging suit, was curled on a wooden captain's chair recounting the Halloween affair in rich detail between sips of coffee and drags on cigarettes.

Joan Enright, a small-boned blonde with a pixie haircut and enormous liquid brown eyes, was alternately laughing and ohhing and ahhing over the incident while she lifted and studied Virginia's hair from various angles. "I think the perfect solution is cellophaning," she announced, turning at once into the consummate professional.

At Virginia's raised brow Joan smiled and gave her shoulder a comforting squeeze. "I'll strip the color from selected strands all over your head. By using temporary rinses we can make you a blonde or brunette at will."

She took a comb and small precision scissors from the pocket of her green uniform. "You've got great hair, with a natural wave. I'm going to shape it and trim off the split ends. You'll still be able to pin it up, but for a different, glamorous look just set it on electric rollers or rag curlers and you'll end up with that sexy tousled look."

Joan redirected her gaze at Diane. "I'm free tomorrow night. Want a little help turning Cinderella into Playmate of the Year?"

"Great!" she exclaimed, unwinding her legs to move alongside Joan. "What about a manicure?" Diane lifted and examined Virginia's fingers, frowning at the uneven nails and the split cuticles. "We can treat them tonight and polish them tomorrow." She peered at Virginia's ashen complexion. "I think a facial too."

"There're some new makeup samples at the shop I'll bring home," Joan contributed, her growing eagerness radiating from her pert features. "I'm really getting excited. It's like giving birth!" She lifted Virginia's chin and grinned into shell-shocked blue eyes. "When we get through with you tomorrow night, you won't recognize yourself."

It took less time than that. On the stroke of midnight Virginia was amazed to see a blonde reflected in the looking glass. Despite the lack of cosmetics the shining spill of hair radiated brilliant streaks of molten gold and shimmered under a seduction of moonbeams.

Then suddenly the sun and stars were washed away by a sober brunette rinse. But professional artistry had changed the originally mouse-colored hair into soft, fluid waves that reflected the mysterious depths of pousse-café.

Virginia had become quite fond of Roger. She always knew what he was thinking; he reacted to her every suggestion and followed her every move. It was very flattering.

True, he was the strong, silent type and rather predictable. Silent because his voice box was lying in little pieces on the workbench; strong because his muscles, joints, and bones were steel, visible through an acrylic body; and predictable because Roger was a robot whose behavior was determined by microchips programmed by Virginia.

Roger had yet to acquire the surface coat of human-looking, synthetic skin, hair and facial movements that would turn him into an audioanimatronic marvel who would dazzle Disney World visitors. But soon, using sophisticated, almost science-fiction techniques and biological electronic implants, Roger would be as charming and personable as any android could be.

Virginia patted the robot's cheek, then let her eyes slide to her colleague's empty desk. It was easy to understand Roger's makeup—not so with Alex Braddock. Alex was infinitely more complex.

He had spent the last four days extolling in great detail the plans he had made for his impending date with Ginger. Here it was past noon on the *big day,* and the man had yet to mention her. What nerve! Especially when Virginia had gone through so many sleepless nights and indecisive days, not to mention personal expense and humbling, to make sure Ginger would appear.

Finally she couldn't stand the suspense anymore and decided to start the ball rolling herself. Positioned at her desk, hand on the telephone, Virginia waited for Alex to step through the air lock.

"Oh, darn!" Her hand rattled the receiver. "Alex, you just missed her." Virginia's voice was deceptively calm, belying the erratic pulse beating beneath the collar of her kelly green sweater.

"And whom did I just miss?" he inquired, his smooth forehead furrowed in confusion.

"Ginger." She smiled at him, her blue eyes wide and guileless. The lies rolled off her tongue as easily as they had in high school. "She just got in from the airport. I told her how insistent you were about tonight." Virginia picked up the Rubik's Cube™ that doubled as a paper weight. "She's very flattered. She's going to take a nap to conquer the jet lag, and she'll be ready at eight."

Alex started to say something, then checked himself. He slid his hands into the pockets of his charcoal slacks and sauntered over to her desk. "I hope this isn't going to complicate matters for us." His eyes reflected the steel tones in his pewter-colored shirt.

"I . . . I don't understand." The lilt in her voice faded as her blue eyes blinked questioningly.

"Well," he paused, choosing his words with care as he settled his hip on the desk corner. "We've become such good friends, and we work so well together . . ." Alex stopped, his face inches from hers. "My relationship with Ginger is destined to be more . . . um . . . intimate. It's just her nature."

Virginia's long fingers began to twist the multicolored puzzle squares in order. "I gather you don't think I have the same *nature*?" came her acidic rejoinder.

Alex shrugged and merely smiled, watching with interest as two sides of the cube already formed a solid color.

"I hazard a guess, Alex," Virginia continued in a rather belligerent tone, "that you'll find an evening with Ginger totally beneath your intellect, your patience, and your endurance. I think I mentioned before, Ginger runs through men the way most people eat potato chips—one after the other." She slammed the realigned puzzle on the desk. "That's *her* nature."

"Maybe I'm conceited enough to think I can change her," he said, a philosophical look crossing his lean features.

"You're right." Virginia stood up. "You are conceited."

His deep, vibrant laugh echoed around the lab. "What will you be doing tonight?"

"Not cramping your style!" she countered on a brusque note. Virginia walked around the desk back to the work table. "I'm going to work on Roger, here. I think I can have him talking in a more natural tone."

Alex looked at the cluttered workbench. "That looks like an all night job." He rubbed his chin, then in an expressionless voice added, "I'm coming in later tomorrow to try the solar pack. Now I'll have Roger's talking to keep me company."

Virginia cast him a sidelong glance, her fingers curled around a precision screwdriver. "I'm sure Roger's conversation will prove more intelligent than Ginger's."

It was almost six when Alex hung up his lab coat and packed his briefcase. Virginia, still engrossed in reassembling tiny electrodes, mumbled a cryptic good-bye.

When the air-lock door hissed closed, she exhaled a pent-up breath and smiled. She had less than two hours to complete her metamorphosis. Reaching into the bench drawer, Virginia pulled out a preassembled voice pack and fit it neatly into the robot's chest. She double-checked it, then pulled the plug on Roger's chatter.

The phone rang. Diane's voice rushed into her ear. "Alex's car just nosed past the security guard. Wash your hair, and I'll be there in a minute."

Golden highlights were poured and combed through her freshly shampooed hair. With infinite care Diane rolled the strands on rag curlers while Virginia deftly applied plum polish to her nails.

Head covered by a scarf, hands and fingers held stiff to protect the new enamel, Virginia slid into the passenger's seat of the yellow VW for the fifteen-minute drive to the apartment.

"I thought Alex would never leave," Diane breathed, pulling into the high-speed lane. "Joan called. She's got a hot bubble bath ready and is whipping up an egg facial."

"I don't think I can do it." Virginia swallowed the flood of saliva that poured into her mouth. "Look at me. I'm shaking!" She held her hands out for inspection. "I'm not even sure Alex believes there are two of us!" Her voice splintered.

"Stop it!" Diane ordered angrily. "That's your whole problem. You end up convincing yourself that you can't do something before you even try." She cast Virginia a disgusted look. "Do you ever say 'can't' when you're working on a project? No! You put all your energies into your work. Now it's time to put them into yourself.

"I want you to take a deep breath, lean your head back, and close your eyes. Go on." Her gaze left the slow-moving traffic long enough to ensure Virginia was following directions. "Sex appeal depends on self-appreciation. Think about all your accomplishments. Think how they've helped society." Diane paused; her voice underwent a subtle, soothing change.

"Remember Halloween night. Remember the laughter, the fun, the romance. Think how great you looked in those new clothes: how they accented your body, enhanced your femininity. Think how wonderful your hair looked, shiny and sparkling with light. You're going to make an impression that will dazzle. You'll cause a stir—you'll finally tap your potential.

"Repeat after me," Diane ordered. "I am a sensuous, sexy, alluring, vibrant, witty woman who is going to enjoy tonight to the fullest."

Virginia repeated it all the way home, repeated it in the elevator, repeated it while Joan smoothed on a facial, then ten minutes later as her makeup was being applied. It wasn't until she had marinated in a tub of scented frothy water and consumed two fingers of brandy that she really began to believe it.

Lolling in the fragrant water, an earthy Lou Rawls serenade drifting in from stereo speakers in the living room, Virginia's attitude began to change.

Plum-dazzled fingertips and toenails winked like jewels against the white blanket of bubbles. The warm water flowed like silk over her sensuous, sleek curves. She was reveling in the pampering and enjoying the crescendo of excitement building inside her.

It was as if her entire body formed an erogenous zone. She felt crisp and sassy. Loose and nonchalant. Exotic and stimulating.

All thoughts of driving Alex away by being boring, stupid, and shallow were replaced by the knowledge she could be a sensuous, cosmopolitan woman. A woman who would spark a man's appetite—a woman who would be the consummate aphrodisiac.

Suddenly Virginia found she was anxious to get dressed and have her hair combed. And more than that, she was anxious for Alex to arrive, anxious for his reaction.

Diane and Joan looked at each other, shook hands, and were visibly in awe of their creation. Their creation could hardly tear herself away from the mirror when the doorbell rang.

CHAPTER SIX

When Virginia opened the door, anticipation was replaced by reality. She did what she had wanted to do all week.

"Darling Bandit!" Taking his hands, she pulled him into the apartment. Virginia ignored Alex's overwhelmed, paralyzed silence, letting her curvaceous anatomy speak to his rugged body.

"I thought I'd never see you again," she breathed, diamond-bright eyes brazenly fastened on his stunned features. Her fingers lifted the thick waves of silver hair that highlighted his temples before pushing his head the scant few inches needed for more intimate connections.

Her tongue teased apart his lips, caressed even white teeth, then probed further into the delicious recesses of his mouth. She savored the taste of him as if he were aged wine, her fingertips exploring his freshly shaven jaw before moving on to torment his earlobe.

Her behavior was guided by her own
own desires. She was finding pleasure

without shame, enjoying the role of relentless seductress.

Back arched, she reveled in the sensuous penetration his rougher black suit material made against her delicate violet silk evening pants. The taste of his mouth, the crisp, assertive scent of his skin, the sureness of his touch, made her glad she had kept the fantasy alive.

Her excitement aroused him. Alex felt the need to take charge and found no barriers. He pressed her submissive body closer, her femininity branding him with her womanly imprint.

His lips were hard and demanding, his tongue a tenacious predator that plundered the lush treasure of her mouth. His hands sought to conquer every enticing inch of skin visible beneath the skimpy metal-mesh halter.

"Still the passionate Rabbit," came his rasping whisper, his warm breath moving the slender silver leaf that dangled from her earlobe.

"Ummm." The sound was a low, throaty purr. Virginia straightened his striped tie and neatened the collar on his granite-toned shirt. "Am I all that you remembered, Alex?" Her gaze locked into his, her attitude pure coquette.

He was hypnotized by kohl-rimmed eyes that looked like a clear mountain stream variegated with violets. "Perhaps even more," Alex admitted, reaching out to playfully tug spun gold curls that fell in a tumbled cascade to her collarbone.

A delighted laugh escaped her full plum-glossed

lips. "That's wonderful!" She clapped her hands like a giddy child, virtually intoxicated with the success of her sleight of hand.

"What about you?" Alex inquired, his large hands curving around her slender upper arms. "Am I what you expected?" His gray eyes left her glowing face to follow the breathtaking, plunging neckline on the meager silver halter. He became mesmerized by the luscious hollow between her full breasts.

She kissed his fingertips, then pressed them against her lips. "Darling Alex, you're all that I desire." Virginia had meant to blend the words with an enchanting giggle, but instead they came out like a sworn statement.

Black mascared lashes fluttering in discomfort, she pulled away. "And what delights does this evening hold?" She moved to retrieve her purse and oriental-style jacket.

Alex followed her provocative movements. The fluid trousers clung to her firm, rounded derriere and draped long, sleek legs. The snaky metal halter absorbed and reflected light, illuminating creamy shoulders and a supple spine. He cleared his throat and shook his head. "I made reservations at the Rendezvous Room, do you know it?"

"No, but I'm sure it will be perfect." Her voice was low and sultry. Slowly and deliberately she walked toward him, a judicious jiggle in each step that made the halter move with scandalous abandon. "I want to know everything about you." Virginia smiled, her eyes glittering with promised pleasures. "All your secrets. All your desires."

Alex took the jacket, guided it over her arms, and adjusted the shoulders. "It seems you and your sister have the monopoly on secrets," he countered smoothly. His cheek nuzzled her neck before turning her around. "I was quite surprised to find twins."

"Virginia told me." She lifted the blond curls free of the mandarin collar. "I never meant to fool you, Alex." She looked at him with wide-eyed gravity, her tongue moistening suddenly dry lips. "In fact, I never expected to see you again." Her fingers crawled up his lapel and tickled his chin. "Am I forgiven?"

He captured her hand and brought it to his mouth. "I could forgive you anything." His lips moved against her palm, and as his teeth nipped the fleshy mound near her thumb he felt her pulse jump.

"Now I want to hear all about your adventures in Japan," Alex announced, holding the door. "What exactly were you modeling?" He cast an amused glance at her tall, well-proportioned figure. "Somehow I don't think it was clothing."

"Actually," her computerlike brain raced through assorted lies while Alex pressed the elevator into action, "I spent the entire week draping myself over various subcompacts at the Tokyo Auto Show." Virginia congratulated herself; it was amazing how inventive one could be in a pinch.

"Is that your usual type of assignment?" he inquired, guiding her through the lobby doors out onto the street.

She gave an inward groan. Alex was annoyingly persistent. "I do mostly catalog work." She favored him with a disarming smile and tucked her hand in the crook of his arm. "I'm sure you've seen me in Sears or Wards or J. C. Penny." Keeping all the lies straight was going to be a monumental feat.

He stopped by a rented maroon Citation. Virginia fluttered her lashes, her fingers stroking his cheek. "I want to hear all about you, Alex," The lambent sheen in her eyes rivaled the glow of the streetlights.

His mouth twisted in a crooked smile as he handed her into the car. "You have a very charming way of terminating a conversation."

Her fingers drummed against her silk-covered thigh. She was determined to control the situation; she was the sorceress in charge of the magic. According to all the how-to books Diane had forced on her, the way to a man's heart was a big plate of seductive flattery, a side dish of verbal foreplay culminating in a mental climax for dessert.

The Rendezvous Room proved to be the perfect place for a seduction. Rich tapestries graced the stucco walls, and amber-lit sconces cast a soft glow over antique furniture, glittering crystal, and pristine white china.

The restaurant was quiet, intimate—no pulsating nightlife. The patrons occupied private carrels, their hushed conversations sparkling with laughter and champagne bubbles. It was a world invaded by the soft sounds of piano, drums, and bass embellishing syncopated jazz, alternating with saxophone and trumpet, which harmonized earthy forties dance tunes.

While the chef served discerning palates the finest haute cuisine in San Pedro, Virginia had Alex well on the road to epicurean delights that were not listed on the sumptuous menu. She was enjoying her sassy new personality and erotic clothes. She played the glamour game with a sure hand.

With the Dom Pérignon and the salad vinaigrette Virginia cooed the usual trivial banalities in a shy playful manner that quite obviously pandered to Alex's ego. Their intimate shared laughter formed an invisible web imprisoning their souls.

During the Coquilles St. Jacques she listened attentively to his stories. Shoulders and thighs touching, her breast pressed against his arm, Virginia found she was once more addicted to the man. Self-assured and dynamic, Alex was able to arouse her mind and set fire to her body like no one ever had.

Between the mousse au chocolat and brandies served in balloon snifters warmed by candle flame, Alex and Virginia luxuriated in the sensual delight of their two bodies melding together in slow rhythmic movements. Oblivious to the other couples, they focused only on each other, dancing in perfect synchronization to the throbbing melody.

"I'd almost forgotten how perfectly we fit together," he murmured, his fingers toying with her golden-veined curls.

Virginia snuggled closer, her lush curves filling in the rugged angles on his masculine frame. Her hands slid beneath his jacket, pressing into the satiny shirt material. The heat of his flesh echoed the blistering fire that was her blood. "The last time we danced it was on a balcony beneath the stars. We were hidden behind costumes and masks." Her cheek rubbed against his neck, her senses assaulted by spicy cologne.

"I still prefer the seclusion of that balcony." Alex's voice was low and vibrant. "But I like the honesty of tonight. No costumes, no masks, no illusions." His firm hands moved with languid abandon down the enticing expanse of bare skin to settle low on her spine.

Virginia swallowed and shifted uncomfortably. Tonight was a bigger illusion than Alex could ever have imagined! But in that illusion came the confidence and security she so desperately needed. Didn't everyone project a false aura? Wasn't everyone something other than they pretended to be? Maybe not so brazen, but life was full of illusions: they were needed to compensate for grim reality.

Virginia knew her feelings were honest, her actions genuine. When she spoke, the words were truthful and from the heart. "Alex," she pulled back slightly. The mood lights on the ceiling reflected off her metal halter and into her eyes. She looked dazzled by diamonds. "I am all that you see, all that you feel. Nothing more, nothing less."

He stared into her radiant features. "I want nothing more. You are everything that I desire."

They danced the night away, only succumbing to the outside world when the trumpet player finally cased his horn and the patient, bovine maître d' continually cleared his throat while the busboys began tabling the chairs for the cleaning crew.

At some point during the evening Virginia had misplaced her original intentions. She had meant to annoy Alex with practiced stupidity; she had meant to masquerade as a vapid coquette; she had meant to appear artificial and shallow. But she had been none of those things.

Virginia felt strangely possessed and deliciously stimulated by her own femininity. Gone was the scientist who dealt in absolutes and felt the necessity to dissect tangibles.

Tonight she celebrated an exquisitely pleasurable range of emotions that were impossible to interpret. And, to be honest, she wanted to savor them rather than analyze them.

The shy, awkward, introspective feelings that had controlled her for so many years had disappeared. Virginia felt content, relaxed, and renewed. Barriers had tumbled; reserves had been pushed aside; and inhibitions were shed. The loss of all excited and stimulated, rather than depressed and frightened.

She refused to make sense of her actions. She refused to acknowledge the danger signals that drifted and darted in her conscience. She concentrated on Alex and the ultimate enjoyment he gave her.

The erotic atmosphere created by her heightened senses echoed in every pore and screamed for release. Virginia decided not to squander one precious second. When Alex unlocked the apartment door, her fingers entwined with his. "I'm not going to let you go yet." Her provocative invitation was readily accepted: they entered the dimly lit living room together.

Virginia found she was anxious to sample the rich reservoir of pleasure contained within Alex. Her body spoke its lines; the unconstructed clothes draped and moved enticingly against her lithe curves. Her come-hither glance bridged a gap of silence that permeated the surroundings.

She enjoyed being brazen; she enjoyed being bold. Plum-tinted toes curled inside the delicate silver evening sandals. She wasn't sure who was going to enjoy the seduction the most.

Alex watched her every move. He was fascinated and hypnotized. Very content to let this golden-haired temptress transport him to paradise.

Virginia tossed her jacket on the velour ottoman, then proceeded to remove Alex's. She continued the striptease, unknotting and pulling his striped silk tie free. Then slowly, deliberately, she released the buttons on his shirt.

Adrenaline pumped through her veins, sending the blood racing, her breathing coming f[illegible] heavier. Black pupils dominated her diam[illegible] irises and fastened hungrily onto Alex's passion-dark eyes. Her left hand pushed aside his shirt, her fingers splayed against his broad chest, tangling in the curly mat of dark hair.

Virginia's right hand lifted the sensuous fall of hair from her neck. Her fingers found the thin silver ribbon that suspended the mesh halter and pulled the restraining bow. The halter fell, leaving her naked to the waist.

The shadowy light cast her silhouette in an ethereal glow. Alex slid his hands lightly up her slender arms to her creamy shoulders. "You are so very beautiful." His hoarse whisper and ragged breathing expressed the tightly leashed control that was ready to snap.

In a momentary suspension of time, with mutual unspoken consent, they drew together like magnets. Virginia gave in to herself and began to respond freely to her feelings. Her needs consumed her the instant Alex's mouth devoured her lips.

Mouths, lips, and tongues joined in explorative maneuvers, provoking and stimulating. Sensations began to build inside Virginia. Her skin felt hot and tingly, shot through with delicious currents that snaked slowly from her stomach down her inner thigh.

Her fingers made erotic squiggles along his rugged torso. Muscles flexed beneath his hair-roughened flesh as she found his erect nipple buried beneath a furry mat. Her smooth fingernail tormented the masculine toughness.

Alex's hands languidly stroked her supple spine, pressing into the creamy, silken skin. His calloused fingers nudged her body chemistry into greater action. Virginia freed her lips. She kissed his straight nose, his strong chin and his Adam's apple. His responding quiver of pleasure enticed her.

She grew bolder, running her tongue lingeringly down the cord of his neck across his chest to his left breast. His flesh was firm and slightly salty, his heart pounded the frantic rhythm of her own.

Alex's fingers blazed a tantalizing trail along her jaw, followed the curve of her shapely neck to the scented valley between her breasts. He rained kisses on her face and neck. He bent his head; his large hand cupped her full breast; his thumb teased the flushed, swollen peaks. The subtle nuances of her perfume stimulated his appetite. His hungry mouth lowered to taste the aroused tips.

Fluttery, pulsating sensations invaded the nucleus of her sexuality. Virginia became lost in physical pleasure. Her throaty moans of aroused abandon intoxicated Alex. He dropped to one knee, his warm mouth bathing the heated flesh of her stomach, his tongue finding a home in her navel.

Anxious for more, without losing bodily contact, they found their way to the massive modular sofa. The cream velour moved sensuously beneath Virginia's bare skin while Alex's virile length provided more provocative friction.

His dark hair felt like silk against her flushed breasts; his lips toured the velvet swells. Her fingernail teased his earlobe and made delicate little forays inside the sensitive drum.

Virginia's right hand slid below his belt. Her fingers toyed with the metal zipper pull while her palm stroked the growing hardness beneath the taut material of his trousers. His growl of pleasure acted like an aphrodisiac, intensifying her own carnal desires.

"Alex, darling, I want you so very badly." Her words tumbled in a frenzied rush. Slow, seductive foreplay had accelerated into the highest pitch of ecstasy.

A door scraped open; light flooded the hallway; a minute later the definitive sound of a toilet flushing invaded their intimate world.

Alex looked down at her, his forehead and eyes mirroring bewildered confusion. Virginia's own eyes grew wide with surprise. Then realization hit her. She was, after all, supposed to be sharing the apartment with her twin. The hallway light snapped off, a door slammed, and with it came the rapid descent of their mood.

"I'm afraid we must have woken my sister." Virginia managed the lie as deftly as she managed the truth: the latter seemed to occur less frequently these days.

He stared into her guileless features for a long moment. "I had forgotten about—Virginia." He shook his head to clear it, then levered himself off the sofa.

"I think it would be less embarrassing if I just

left." Alex picked up his jacket and headed for the door. Pausing to straighten his shirt, he looked back at the sensuous, tumbled woman still lying amid the cream cushions, and then picking up his jacket, he let himself out.

Ginger or Virginia—one sensible and efficient; one alluring and mysterious. Both were making his world delightfully off-balance and unexpectedly pleasurable.

It took quite a while for Virginia's strength to return. While she was less than satiated physically, she was more than satisfied with the evening.

She found no shame in her actions. No shame in being a woman with needs and desires. No shame in asking a man she was deeply attracted to to fulfill them.

Her body still vibrated from Alex's touch. There would be no cold shower for her—his caresses and kisses were too precious to be washed away.

Refastening the halter, Virginia strolled into her bedroom. The bedside Tensor light illuminated two women clad in lounging robes, playing cards scattered over the blue chenille spread, and a pair of expectant faces. Leaning against the door frame, Virginia looked at Diane and Joan, a Cheshire-cat grin spreading across her still flushed features.

"Well?" came their breathless chorus.

"Well what?" She was being deliberately obtuse.

Diane looked at Joan. They both reached for bed pillows and tossed the soft punches at her. Laughing, she easily batted them to the sea-toned carpet.

"Did we convince Alex that there was another person here?" Diane demanded, pushing the cards in a haphazard pile to make room for Virginia.

"You certainly did," came her matter-of-fact retort. Her lashes shaded her shining eyes. "Although I wish you hadn't picked that particular moment to play chaperon."

"Ohhh." The two-part harmony was tinged with the wisdom of affairs of heart.

Virginia collapsed on the edge of the platform bed, elbows on her silk-covered knees, face resting on her palms. "Maybe I should be grateful that you did interrupt." A myriad of confused feelings assaulted her, tumbling her from previous ecstatic heights.

Diane and Joan scrambled across the mattress on their knees to her side. "What's the matter?" Joan asked quietly, tugging her brown plaid robe free of her feet. "Wasn't Alex what you expected? Was the evening a dud?"

Diane patted Virginia's shoulder comfortingly. "Was he a fake? Was he dull and boring without his work to talk about? Was he less than the Bandit on the balcony?"

"I was the fake," she returned on a glum note. "I had the whole evening planned in my mind. I was supposed to be dull and boring. I was supposed to be stupid and giddy and nauseating." Virginia looked from Joan to Diane and shook her blond curls. "I'm afraid I didn't do any of those things. Instead of turning Alex off, I turned him on." She swallowed past the lump in her throat and looked down at her clenched hands. "I didn't have to fake a damn thing. It just came naturally."

"So what's the problem?" Diane laughed, rubbing her hands on her red terry lounger with delight. "You've got him hooked, and you've got yourself feeling terrific."

"Ginger has him hooked. *Ginger* feels terrific," Virginia retorted, her harsh tone suddenly turning brittle. "I feel miserable."

A florist's messenger arrived early Saturday morning. Inside the pale pink box were six perfect red roses and a card that read: "Each delicate blossom echoes a passionate letter of your name—Alex." A veil of sadness cloaked Virginia as she stroked a satiny bloom against her cheek. Ginger's was the only name with six letters!

When the telephone rang later that same afternoon, she instinctively knew it would be Alex. But she was ready for him, having spent the better part of an hour composing yet another tangle of lies that would make Ginger vanish.

It was a trembling hand that lifted the receiver, and in the few seconds it took to reach her ear, Virginia's resolve was shattered under a barrage of carnal memories. Instead of answering with her usual crisp "Dr. Farrell," a sultry, languid soprano drifted across the lines and eagerly accepted Alex's invitation to dinner.

She wore a slim, tomato-red silk jump suit, its cowl neck draped to hazardous depths, her slender waist accented with a gold obi sash. Alex was delighted with her choice, saying she surpassed the red roses in beauty.

They went back to the Rendezvous Room. They suppered on delicate shrimp crepes and fed each other fresh pineapple and succulent orange sections dipped in a bittersweet chocolate fondue. They danced continuously and dallied till the wee hours over warmed brandies. Laughing, talking, sharing, enjoying each other.

When Alex brought her home, he seemed reluctant to come in and disturb "Virginia." She had to make do with a handful of kisses that more than fanned their mutual passion.

For the next ten days the Rendezvous Room became "their" place. They sat at "their" private table, and the musicians played "their" favorite melodies. Whispered love words, kisses, and caresses were no longer enough. The flames of desire were burning out of control, and the inevitable was only a matter of time and place.

Alex apologized, for he was staying with the Quimbys, and Virginia found she was contemplating sending "herself" on a trip so that "Ginger" and Alex could have the apartment.

In the end it was "Ginger" who left. "She got a call from her agent and is off to the Bahamas doing a bathing-suit spread for the week," Virginia announced the weekend before Thanksgiving. "She asked me to apologize for breaking your dinner date."

Sitting Indian-style on the lab floor working on the robot's hands, she looked up at Alex through the clear tops of her magnifying glasses and waited. He merely nodded and went on installing the solar battery. She had hoped he would ask her to be a replacement—but he didn't.

Maybe it was for the best, Virginia rationalized, selecting a precision screwdriver and returning her attention to Roger the robot. Their evenings were becoming too intense, and the duplicity involved was making her a nervous wreck.

"The left hand and the right hand are not supposed to know what each was doing," she had told Diane over a coffee and toaster waffle breakfast. During the day she was constantly on guard not to repeat anything said the previous evening. At night she had to remember not to know what went on at the lab. Virginia shook off her confused thoughts—both of her identities could use a week's rest.

Still, it made her angry that even though they worked side by side and shared their lunch hour, Alex failed to see her as a woman. They had become the best of friends. He asked and valued her opinions, but it was all work-related—no hint of ever turning it into the personal exchange he was having with Ginger.

Alex hadn't even noticed the changes she had made in her appearance. Gone was the severe bun and unadorned complexion. Virginia had side-parted her brown waves, letting them soften her squarish features, while basic cosmetics subtly enhanced her eyes, cheeks, and lips. She had even purchased more colorful, better-fitting additions to her wardrobe and actually started wearing dresses on the days she did her reports.

Granted, it was nothing as dramatic as her "Ginger look," but then, she wasn't out to seduce Alex—was she? Lately Virginia felt more competitive with Ginger. But they were both one and the same—weren't they?

Alex watched Virginia as she made some final adjustments to Roger's right hand. Her expertise amazed him. She had been able to make the robot speak and move in a frighteningly human fashion. Now Roger was even able to write in a decorative calligraphic script.

"You really astound me." Alex put his thoughts into words as he gave Virginia a helping hand off the floor. "Your work is brilliant. You've finished this project over a month early and far surpassed everyone's expectations."

She brushed off the seat of her tan cords and smiled at him. "I was just lucky," she returned modestly. She could feel the heat rushing to her face and began to fiddle with the rolled sleeves on her madras shirt. "I spent last summer in Tokyo working for a toy company on many of these same problems. I ended up learning more than I contributed. The Japanese lead the world in robotics technology."

"That's quite a coincidence."

Virginia blinked at him. "What is?"

"That both you and Ginger have been to Japan,"

he returned evenly, snapping the faceplate over the battery terminal.

She turned toward the workbench, trembling fingers picking and discarding various instruments. "We both travel a lot. It's not that much of a coincidence." Virginia took a deep controlling breath, scolding herself over the slip.

Alex gave a little laugh. "Actually it's the only thing you two do seem to have in common," he continued, his voice and manner quite nonchalant. "It really amazes me just how different you both are."

Needle-nose pliers clattered against the table. "I don't think we are *that* different," Virginia grated, her lips thinning in anger.

"Oh, now, yes. Yes you are," he said quickly. Alex opened the control panel on the robot's chest and pulled out a collection of colored wires. "Ginger is more . . . um . . . earthy. Do you know what I mean?"

Virginia cleared her throat and squared her shoulders. "No, no, I don't," came her clipped answer. She still refused to turn around, pretending to be busy with the schematic notations.

Alex cast a sidelong amused glance at her military posture. "Well, she is very natural. She says what she feels, does whatever gives her pleasure, and in doing that, she gives others pleasure."

"Of course, I'm just the opposite."

"I didn't say that."

"The implication was there," she said in a tightly leashed voice. Virginia plastered a sweet smile on her face and turned to confront Alex. "You really shouldn't jump to such conclusions about people, Alex." His raised eyebrows made her continue. "You only know me from nine to five. But what I'm like from five to midnight might surprise you."

"A chameleon?" He looked like the thought appealed to him. "Maybe I did judge on circumstantial evidence." Alex went back to connecting matching colored wires.

Virginia held her breath. Perhaps this was a breakthrough? Maybe now Alex would turn to her. But by Wednesday she realized there was only one woman for Alex—Ginger.

CHAPTER SEVEN

"What's this?" Closing the apartment door, Diane stared at the leather Pullman sitting in the foyer.

"A suitcase." Virginia didn't bother to look up from transferring the contents of her tan clutch into a brown-leather shoulder bag.

"I can see that," she retorted with heavy sarcasm. Diane took a deep breath, walked over to the dining room table, and grabbed Virginia by the shoulders. "What's going on? I came down to tell you that Thanksgiving dinner will be ready at three instead of one, and now I find this!"

Virginia turned away, her fiery cheeks betraying her guilt. "I forgot about tomorrow. I'm sorry. I'm not coming." She freed her arms and began to count the money in her billfold.

"This has something to do with Alex," Diane hissed. "What happened?" she demanded. After getting a noncommittal shrug she plunked her size-five body on the corner of the suitcase. "No one gets out of here alive until I know what, when, where, and why."

"All right." Virginia stuffed her wallet in her purse, closed it, then threw it on the table. "I can't take it anymore." She stood in front of Diane, hands on hips. "You said play the game for fun. Take it for all it's worth." Virginia took a deep breath. "Well, it's not fun. It wasn't really fun from the start, and now there's more at stake than a silly masquerade."

She paced up and down the slate foyer, her rust suede skirt beating against the back of her calves. "I should have stuck with my original resolution to make 'Ginger' look like animated Silly Putty. But I didn't. Ginger was too good, and Alex has fallen in love with her."

"But that's wonderful," Diane interrupted, her blue eyes lighting up in excitement. "Or," she added after a moment's hesitation, "don't you want a permanent relationship?"

"Diane." Virginia rubbed the center of her forehead with her palm, her fingers pushing back a loose brown wave. "Don't you understand? Alex doesn't love me. He loves Ginger."

"You are Ginger."

"No. No, I'm not."

Diane shifted uncomfortably and tried to ignore the itchy prickles that jolted her skin. "Now listen, Virginia." She cleared her throat and made her voice as soothing as possible. She felt like a psychiatrist dealing with a patient. "There is only one of you. You're . . . you're . . ." She brightened. "You're like Clark Kent: mild-mannered reporter by day and Superman by night."

"What happens when Superman balks at being Clark Kent?" Virginia asked, her expression totally serious. "Right now I don't know which is the real me." She picked up a matching suede jacket and slid it over a beige sleeveless knit sweater. "I'm going to spend four days trying to find myself." Virginia held up her hand. "I know that's a well-worn cliché, but in this instance enormously apropos. I'm not sure which one of us will be coming back—if I come back at all."

Diane scooted past and grabbed her purse. "All right, maybe you do need to get away," she rationalized. "But, please, at least tell me where?"

Virginia smiled at her. "You've been the best friend I could ever have. I don't want to lose you." She gave Diane a quick hug, then easily regained possession of her shoulder bag. "I'm going to head down the Coast. La Jolla, I think. A nice motel room overlooking the sea."

"Will you at least call and tell me which motel?" Diane pleaded, trotting behind her toward the door. "I'm really worried. I'm afraid you'll run away."

"I have been running." Virginia picked up her suitcase and opened the door. "I've been hiding from the truth. Now I've got to face it; take a good, hard look at myself and decide what's what." She walked out.

The Pacific coast was rockier and rougher than the Atlantic, but southern California was as warm and sunny as Florida in mid-November. La Jolla, Virginia discovered, had a magnificent coastline. It reminded her of the French Riviera. The waves were not so turbulent; the soft, sandy beach was wide and practically free of boulders.

Today the bright blue sky, with dollops of whipped-cream clouds, stretched all around, flattening into the gray-misted horizon. With the warm tide ruffling between her toes and a much-loved beach firm beneath her feet, Virginia found she had to swallow back a wave of homesickness for her own cottage in Cocoa Beach.

Shading her eyes, she looked back toward the sun-blistered coral cabin that had been home for the last three days. The Wayfarer's Inn proved true to its name, providing travelers with a tranquil hideaway and a private beach inhabited by sea gulls and an occasional surf fisherman. It was the perfect place to think.

At first Virginia had balked at thinking, but meditation and water seemed to be wed. The cherished ocean with its infinite billowing waves spoke to the troubled sea that was her mind and soul. At night the serene ocean carpet glowed under magenta and copper sunsets like a crucible of light and heat. The omnipotent sea was its usual soothing self, and Virginia became convinced that everything could be resolved.

Virginia lifted the prairie skirt well above her knees as she ventured deeper into the warm, frothy surf. A smile curved her lips. In a way the skirt was a duplicate of her own split personality. The serious wheat-colored cotton, with a thin blue-green plaid, covered a frivolous, ruffled underslip. "Wasn't it the same with Virginia-Ginger?"

There were things about Ginger that she liked and had decided to keep. Her free hand lifted the salt-damp curls that plastered her cheek. She liked the blond hair: it made her complexion look healthier, and it lifted her spirits. That morning she had permanently assigned the bottle of brown rinse to the garbage. Virginia would stay blond.

She also liked her glamorous evening wardrobe. The clothes were frankly feminine, frankly alluring. Her figure was good, and the sensuous fabrics made her feel good. They would stay too.

And she liked Ginger's "earthy" quality. No, Virginia rationalized, it wasn't because *he* liked it. What was wrong with saying what you felt and doing what you wanted—as long as it didn't hurt anyone? Too many people were popping Valium and antacids just because they kept their true feelings bottled up. And for what—a nervous breakdown?

What was so wrong with a woman being the aggressor? Where was it written that only men could be bold and adventurous? If a man was so insecure that he couldn't accept a woman who spoke her mind and handled her own destiny, who needed him?

Virginia also began to value her own intelligence. Why should she depreciate her God-given talent? She had already contributed to society and felt fortunate enough to have the capability to give even more. No more apologies for her brains, for her inventiveness, or for her discoveries. Women weren't relegated to home and hearth anymore. Equality was going to have to be accepted and embraced.

As for Alex? Despite the sun an icy chill permeated her thin beige T-shirt. Bumps prickled her skin, sending her back toward shore. Alex. He had been the major stumbling block for the last seventy-two hours.

Virginia used her big toe to carve his name into the wet sand just a hair's breadth out of reach of the tide. Out of reach? Yes, that was Alex. And when he knew the truth—would he feel ridiculed, betrayed, outraged, fooled? All of those? And why shouldn't he?

But she had never set out to fool him. From the beginning she was driven by initial attraction and infatuation, then later desire turned into something deeper. Love? But love had always been elusive, and there was no reason to think fate would smile this time.

Virginia decided to go back, confront Alex, and let him decide. If he found it too difficult to work with her, if the sight of her made him sick, she would have Briarcliff send a replacement. She'd go back to Florida for a much-needed rest. She'd always have Alex. Vivid, rich, tangible—indelible memories that stained her life for all time.

A squadron of sea gulls broke form, hovered, then glided down on the sand around her. Their curved beaks intently assaulted the tide for minute plankton to satisfy temporarily their never-ending hunger. Watching them, Virginia realized she too could use a bite to eat, although lunch at the inn would be considerably more appetizing.

She picked her way through the pearl-gray scavengers, who staunchly refused to acknowledge her presence. Then, quite suddenly, the air exploded with black-tipped wings and raucous cries. Quickly she turned to see what had frightened the feeding gulls. Virginia found it was Alex.

She stared at him, swallowing convulsively, sea blue eyes locked onto gray ones. Alex looked quite invincible and formidable, very much the Bandit, his lean muscular physique cloaked all in black.

"Diane told me where to find you." He readily provided the answer to one unspoken question.

Her tongue circled her teeth trying to find enough moisture to wet her lips. She wondered just whom Alex had come to see? No! The pretending had to stop. Anger replaced anxiety; Virginia found she was quite defensive. "Well, Alex, you lucked out—you've found both of us at once."

"At last!" His words were tinged with relief.

"Oh, no. No!" Her eyes widened, then narrowed into piercing sapphire slits. "You mean you've known all along?"

Alex smiled and nodded. "I've known from the very beginning." He crossed his arms over his chest, amusement registering in his eyes. "Although that first night," he shook his head, scratching his chin reminiscently, "you really stunned me. When I left you in the lab, you were a serious, dedicated brunette —all work and no play. A few hours later I had a sensuous, fun-loving blond bundle catapulted into my arms." Alex smiled at her again.

Virginia's fingers curled into impotent fists. "You knew all the time," she repeated again, still not believing his confession. "And I've been worried sick that you'd think I was playing you for the fool. And all the while . . ." Her voice trailed off miserably.

"I enjoyed every minute of it," he told her, his deep voice quite serious. Alex pushed a wind-whipped blond curl off her cheek. "I had never been seduced before. I found it quite enjoyable."

"Of all the low, miserable, conniving, cheap, dirty, disgusting . . . ugh. . . ." She slapped his hand away, her bare foot stomping the wet sand in anger.

"Don't you think that's like the pot calling the kettle black?" Alex arched a dark brow, studying the range of emotions displayed on her sun-kissed features.

She drew herself up, her body rigid with indignation. "Alex Braddock, you don't deserve either one of us." Virginia turned on her heel and stalked up the beach.

"Wait a minute!" Alex shouted, hastily catching up with her. "Virginia." His long legs easily matched her angry strides. "Let's be sensible and talk about this."

"Sensible!" Her voice was shrill, her lips curled in contempt. "I'm surprised you think I could ever be sensible or rational"—her legs increased their speed—"or reasonable or normal." Her toes spewed little clumps of sand in her wake. "I was beginning to doubt my own sanity." Virginia all but shouted at Alex's jogging frame. "And for what? This . . . this utter humiliation!"

"Virginia, please." His large hand was finally able to secure her flailing arm.

She stopped and twisted free. A maelstrom of emotions whirled inside of her. Virginia looked at him, her breasts heaving beneath the thin cotton shirt. "For two cents I'd tell you exactly what I think of you, Alex Braddock." She turned and mounted the ocean-carved rock steps leading to her cottage.

Virginia found an unfamiliar suitcase had invaded her cabin. Her fingers curled around the black-leather handle, but as she moved to toss it out the still open door, Alex's rugged physique blocked her efforts.

One large hand plucked the valise from her numb fingers; the other thrust two copper images of Lincoln under her nose. She stared at the coins for an interminable length of time, their images becoming distorted by the tears that stung her eyes.

The pennies tumbled to the multicolored shag carpet. The masculine hands that had held them slid around her waist, drawing her trembling body against his rock-hard strength.

"In your rush to toss out my suitcase," Alex's voice was low and comforting against her ear, "you failed to notice the eight white roses in the vase on your dresser." His thumb and forefinger c[illegible] her chin, lifting her face level with his [illegible] smiled into her liquid eyes. "Each [illegible] breathes the gift of love to every letter of your name." He closed her eyelids with a kiss, his lips tasting the salty tears that dribbled down her cheeks.

Eight roses—eight letters in Virginia. Not red for passion, but white for love. Her lashes fluttered open, her arms wrapped tightly around his waist. "Alex," Virginia sniffed, her puddled blue gaze brimming with unspoken questions, "I . . . you . . . we . . ." She swallowed the nonsensical words, her shoulders slumping under a mixture of confusion and uncertainty.

"Dr. Farrell." He sounded quite exasperated, but the arms that held her, the hands that caressed her, told a different story. "I love you to distraction. You are the essence of everything that I want, everything that I need. I feel extremely fortunate to have found a composite of all women, packaged in perfection." Alex lowered his head, his mouth seeking to possess hers, when Virginia suddenly pulled away.

She dropped to the edge of the bed. "What must you think of me?" Virginia looked up at him, then down at her hands, her fingers twisted around one another. "What kind of woman must you think I am? I hardly knew you, and I carried on like a . . . a . . ." She couldn't even bring herself to say the coarse names lodged in her throat.

Alex rested his palms on her shoulders, then pushed her backward onto the mattress. "I know all I need to know about you." The anger glittering in his gray eyes matched his harsh tone. "I know that you are the best thing to ever happen to me." His voice softened: "And I know that I'm not going to let you go."

Her hands cradled his face; her body lifted to press against the virile length stretched out across her own. "Alex, I love you." Her hands slid around his neck and pulled his head down. Her lips touched his. "It was love that gave me the strength to show you my true feelings."

"I certainly wouldn't mind if you gave me another demonstration," he whispered. But Alex couldn't wait—his mouth crushed hers with a savage urgency that negated all remaining doubts.

His kisses and caresses sent those familiar sweet sensations moving through her blood to her heart. She savored the loving feelings, with the knowledge that Alex shared them making them infinitely more satisfying.

Virginia found she was suddenly quite impatient and annoyed with the clothes that prevented a more intimate union. Her hands tugged his knit shirt free, pulling it up toward his shoulders. Alex sat up, taking Virginia with him. With obvious reluctance he broke their embrace. But after he finished disposing of his shirt he was delighted to find she had done the same.

They played a little game of quid pro quo—"something for something." Prairie skirt covered twill pants; ruffled slip drifted over shoes and socks; briefs laid claim to apricot satin panties.

Slowly they drew together, Virginia's silken curves conforming against Alex's muscular physique. The fusion of their bodies ignited the persistent embers of passion, flaming them into the essence of love.

Her lips played with his; her teasing tongue darted into his mouth. Her smooth fingernails delicately scratched her initials into his chest.

Alex gave a low groan—his kisses became more than gentle. His mouth plundered her soft lips, claiming ownership of her very breath. His hands flowed down her spine and curved around her firm buttocks.

Alex guided her back onto the bed, her body dissolving into the mattress beneath his sinewy strength. "I love you, Virginia." His words were whispered against her full breasts, as his mouth and tongue teased and licked the taut peaks.

She moaned softly as he ventured lower. His lips and fingers explored the feminine nooks and crannies. The sensuous stimulation of his gentle probings created continuous ripples of ecstasy that washed over her like a languid warm tide.

Virginia pulled his head back to hers. "Alex, I love you so very much." The ache in her voice begged for their mutual fulfillment. Her fingers snaked down his flat-bellied torso, her hand sculpting across the lines of his body.

Alex crouched over her, his eyes locked into hers. He lifted her hips. She eagerly received him—a more joyous connection could not have been imagined. Their physical union formed a complete circle of love.

Her long silken legs entwined around his powerful

hips as the intensity of his passion grew steadily stronger and deeper. Alex knew when to be gentle and when to be rough. His lovemaking was passionate and exhilarating. Her body vibrated with primitive tremors of rapture, her own rhythmic movements synchronized with his.

It was an illusion of unity: they were joined, but their sensations remained their own. Fluttery, pulsating currents racked her body. Passion erupted in a nerve-shattering explosion, and her nails gripped Alex's flesh like claws.

He pulled her tighter, sealing her against him. His body shuddered, the climax to his passion breaking over her like a violent storm—a storm centered deep inside her. Alex rolled over, taking Virginia with him, their perspiration-anointed, satiated bodies still united in the afterglow of love.

"Telling you how much I love you seems very inadequate," Alex murmured huskily, his hands settling low on her spine. He kissed her nose, her chin, her lips. "You make me want to go out and conquer the world. I've looked a lifetime for you." He smiled into her passion-dark eyes. "Will you marry me?"

Virginia blinked at him. "Alex, I never expected . . . you don't have to . . ." She stopped babbling and took a deep breath. "I certainly will!" Her head collapsed against his chest. She felt enormously happy and delightfully intoxicated.

He grinned and rolled her over. "Now that I can call both of you mine," he growled into the softness of her throat, "I think I'll just have to show you again how delighted I am with my fascinating bride-to-be."

"Alex . . ." She peeked at him through fluttering lashes as his lips lowered to her breast. Once again she abandoned herself to Alex's devastating love-making.

The sun was a flaming orange ball, suspended low in the striated blue sky. "We've loved the afternoon away." She yawned sleepily at Alex.

"We still have time to catch a plane to Las Vegas," came his succinct announcement. Alex gave her bare buttocks a playful slap as he slid out of bed and began to hunt for his clothes.

"What?" Virginia sat up, a sensuous, flushed vision amid the tumbled flowered sheets. "Alex, you're crazy!" She blinked in astonishment, watching him pull on his navy briefs. "You want to get married right now? Tonight?"

"Darling"—he walked back and perched on the edge of the bed—"the next time I make love to you, you are going to be my wife." Alex lifted her left hand to his lips, his eyes more eloquent than words.

Virginia took another sip of the aged French champagne, placed the crystal tulip glass on the tile shelf, and uttered her hundredth contented sigh. "I married an incurable romantic." Her head rested against his, blond curls embracing brown.

"A bride belongs in the bridal suite," Alex said matter-of-factly. He picked up a large succulent strawberry, dipped it in powdered sugar, and fed it to Virginia. "Tomorrow we head back to reality." A chuckle escaped him. "I can't wait to see Jerome's reaction when I tell him I'm moving in with my lab partner, who is now my wife."

"Mrs. Alex Braddock." Virginia savored each word. To her they were sweeter than the strawberries, more sparkling than the wine. She sighed again, her soapy hand moving lovingly across her husband's chest.

Stretching a sleek leg, she let her toe readjust the jet action of the whirlpool. The water in the sunken heart-shaped tub erupted into a frothy, bubbly confection. Virginia eyed the serene, satiated couple reflected in the Palace of Versailles mirrored bathroom with smug satisfaction.

Life with Alex would be utopia. Their love was a strong, powerful bond enhanced by mutual respect. They complemented each other, fed each other's needs. It was as if they had achieved a sense of oneness. They truly had the framework for a strong, secure married life.

The sybaritic pink bath, ringed with hypnotic flickering, scented candles, and aromatic incense, proved to be a compelling aphrodisiac. A soft smile played at the corners of Virginia's mouth. She picked up another handful of creamy lather, spreading it over the broad expanse of Alex's powerful torso, and moved to massage his neck and shoulde[illegible] love you," she whispered into his ear, her t[illegible] nipping the lobe.

Alex shifted position. His hands pushed aside the suds, preferring to caress her skin. She felt like silk—glossy and sleek and warm. He could feel his body reacting to the passion only Virginia could so readily ignite.

He pulled her tightly against him. Her satiny stomach and full breasts tantalized his flesh. "I love you so very much." His mouth captured her lips, drinking deeply of their sweetness.

The pulsating, swirling heated bath water enhanced their burgeoning passion. Virginia delighted in the discovery of her inherent sensuality. She had never felt more alive, more womanly, more content, more happy, than right now. With her arms locked around her husband's waist she eagerly let her pliant feminine curves consume her husband's compelling masculinity.

CHAPTER EIGHT

"Is this coffee or mud?" Alex joked. His spoon seemed to be having a great deal of difficulty stirring the thick black liquid.

Virginia peered over the morning newspaper. "I must have used one too many scoops." She smiled at him. "Sorry, darling. It seems you need to use a different amount for every brand in order for it to come out right."

"Why don't you just keep buying the same one?" he asked.

She shrugged and went back to the business news. "I guess I just don't notice what I buy."

Alex pushed back the chair and went to pour the gruesome brew down the sink. "Virginia," his voice called from the kitchen, "this refrigerator is empty." He walked back into the dining room, his hands pulling down the newspaper. "There're no eggs, no bread; the milk has turned into cottage cheese—nothing is in there but a box of baking soda."

"Alex," she chided. "I've been away for five days and never expected to have to feed anyone breakfast when I got back." Virginia stood up and slid her arms around his neck. "We can pick up some groceries tonight." She rubbed her cheek against his smoothly shaven jaw. The spicy scent of his after-shave sent a warm rush of heat through her.

"I'm sorry, darling." Alex kissed the tip of her nose while his hands patted her derriere beneath the batik caftan. "Listen, you better get a move on. Traffic is murder in the mornings."

She sighed. "You're right." She managed to sneak one last kiss, reluctantly leaving his embrace to finish dressing.

"I like being driven to work," Virginia announced an hour later as they walked through the maze of hallways toward the lab. "I made copius notes on the telemetric linkup problem."

"I battled traffic," Alex grumbled, shifting his brown attaché case to his left hand.

"Poor baby!" Virginia cast an amused glance at her husband. Husband—the very word sent a pleasurable shiver down her spine. She still found the events of the past few days difficult to believe. Her eyes rechecked the wide gold band on her left hand, then focused on Alex's rugged profile. He looked inordinately handsome in a cranberry knit shirt and charcoal trousers.

"Alex." Her whisper halted their progress. He eyed her flushed features with rueful suspicion. Virginia's fingers flowed along the curve of his cheekbone, tantalized his lips, before caressing his strong jaw. "Did I ever tell you all the erotic things I thought about doing with you in the lab?"

Noting that the hallway was empty, Alex pushed her against the concrete wall. "At times you can be a very naughty lady." His smoky gaze darkened at the lambent passion glowing in her iridescent blue eyes. "I have a hunch little work is going to get done today."

"I certainly hope not!" Virginia managed to look quite prim, pulling down the sleeves of her dark blue dress and straightening the matching belt. "I'd hate to think the honeymoon was over after forty-eight hours."

An obscenely cheery whistle and the unmistakable sound of footsteps had Alex and Virginia hastily returning to more proper decorum. Jerome Quimby's stocky figure rounded the bend, his hazel eyes brightening at the sight of them.

"I was just down at the lab looking for you." He rocked back on his leather heels, thumbs hooked in his brown vest. "I have a little surprise for you in my office."

Alex winked at Virginia. "Is this our first wedding present?"

"I've got one of those too, but this . . . this is something even more exciting." Jerome gave a gleeful chuckle, enjoying their puzzled looks. "Come along." He scurried ahead of them, his mysterious quips and comments leaving Virginia and Alex shaking their heads in confusion.

"Surprise!" Jerome pushed open his office door. A

burst of flashbulbs blinded Virginia. She jumped backward, grateful for the solid comfort of her husband's steadying grip.

"What is all this, Jerome?" Alex looked at the half-dozen reporters who had lunged to their feet, pencils poised over notebooks.

Jerome held up a stubby hand. "Ladies and gentlemen of the press, may I present this year's National Medal of Science winner in the field of cryogenics—Dr. Virginia Farrell."

Virginia let out a startled gasp. "What! When did this happen? . . . Alex?" She turned, eyes wide with astonishment. Questions erupted from the reporters; flashbulbs exploded. Jerome Quimby pulled Virginia across the room so she could stand between the American flag and the emblem of AVELCOMP Industries.

A reed-thin sandy-haired reporter sidled up to Alex. "What's your connection with the doctor?" he inquired, hoping to scoop his colleagues with an interesting side bar.

"Virginia is my wife."

"Oh? That's swell." He flipped open his notebook. "Listen, Mr. Farrell, how does it feel to be married to—"

"It's Braddock," Alex corrected, his voice sharper than he'd intended.

The reporter shifted a wad of gum around his mouth. "What's Braddock?" He scribbled something on his pad, his eyes and ears sharply tuned to the rest of the assemblage.

"My name. It's Alex Braddock."

The reporter squinted up at him, shook his head, then snapped the page from his note pad. "I thought you said you were her husband. Forget it, Mac." He moved off and pushed his way through to the award winner.

Alex stabbed through the golden-brown crust on the chicken pot pie, a fragrant blast of heat pushing into his face. "When you said there was plenty of food in the freezer, I never expected this." He tossed his fork aside and reached for his wineglass.

"It's delicious." Virginia's elbow nudged his arm. "All those nutritionists at General Foods do a great job," she teased, holding a forkful of bite-size pieces of chicken, carrots, and peas to his lips. "Taste it."

He pushed her hand away. "I'm a meat-and-potatoes man."

"I've got a steak TV dinner in there." She started to slide off her chair.

"Virginia." Alex grabbed her arm, halting any further movement. "*Real* food tastes so much better."

"This is real!" She laughed, giving him a quick kiss.

"Darling." His tone was one of patient forbearance. His hand reached up to pat her blond topknot. "I mean meat from a butcher and french fries made from real potatoes."

Amusement was replaced by apprehension. Virginia blotted her mouth on her napkin, her palms rubbing the panels on her silk flower-strewn kimono.

"You know, Alex, I put in a full day at the lab. I really don't feel like coming home and playing Julia Child." She looked at him, her expression quite serious. "The truth is I can't comprehend even the simplest recipes." She took a deep breath and finished her confession. "Alex, I'm hopeless in the kitchen."

He smiled at her. "I'm not asking for gourmet, darling. What is there to grilling a steak? Slicing a potato? Tossing a salad?" Alex cradled her face between his hands. The pleasant expression that curved his lips was not duplicated in his eyes. "I'm sure the winner of the National Science Medal could manage that."

Virginia swallowed hard. Was she just imagining an underlying bitterness in his voice, a strained, tense look around his mouth and eyes. "Alex." She grasped his hand, her thumb stroking his palm. "You've been awfully quiet all day. That award was a complete surprise. I really think Jerome went overboard with all those interviews. First the newspapers and then those TV cameras." She licked her lips, her voice hesitant. "I hope you didn't feel ig . . . ignored."

"Really, Virginia." Alex pulled his hand free from her grasp. His tone was clipped and brusque, his manner defensive. "I don't know how you got that impression." He drained the rest of the white wine. "I'm very proud of you." Alex picked up his fork and viciously attacked the pot pie. "I told you before how much I admire your work. I don't know what else you expect after all—"

There was a sharp knock on the door, and Diane burst into the apartment. "Wait until you see this!" She was waving the evening newspaper at them while she ran to the small color TV set on the bookcase. "Look . . . look!" She pointed at the immediately visible picture. "You're right there, over Dan Rather's shoulder." Diane turned up the volume to a dangerously high decibel level.

Virginia sprinted to stand next to her. "Oh, God. Look at my hair . . . and that dress." She groaned and hid her face in her hands.

"Will you stop." Diane hushed her, listening to every word the evening news reported. When the brief story was finished, she switched off the set. "I called everyone I knew and told them to watch the news tonight. I thought it would only be on the local station and then, when National announced this—well!" Diane grabbed her by the shoulders. "Aren't you thrilled?" She looked back toward Alex, who was still sitting at the table. "Alex, didn't she look marvelous? And did you see the photograph of that award?"

"Marvelous," Alex agreed, lifting his refilled wineglass in a toastlike gesture.

"I want you to autograph that newspaper," Diane continued, jabbering away at a mile a minute. "Mom couldn't believe it. Of course, she knew you when." She erupted in a burst of giggles. "You know, you should really get a few copies of the paper." She pushed a pen into Virginia's hand. "Alex, your folks will want to see their famous daughter-in-law."

"Famous!" Virginia wrinkled her nose. "I'm hardly that." Nonetheless she wrote her name with artistic flourish. "I do wish I'd had some notice though. I would have worn something different."

Diane gave Virginia's blond topknot a playful tug. "And you were the one I couldn't get into a dress shop with a Mack truck." She slanted a gaze toward the dining room. "Alex, you've just done wonders for her. She's like a caterpillar turned into a butterfly."

Sharp staccato blasts, as if from an air horn, splintered Alex's eardrums. He turned off the shower, thrust his arms into a terry robe, and threw open the bathroom door. Immediately he smelled something burning. The hallway and living room were filled with smoke. He waved his way through it. "Virginia!" he shouted. "Damn it, where are you? Virginia! Are you all right?"

Coughing, tears streaming from smarting eyes, Alex collided with his wife. The broiler pan slid from Virginia's pot-holdered hand and noisily crashed against the white linoleum, sending what appeared to be smoldering lumps of coal scooting across the floor.

"What the hell happened?" Alex sputtered. He groped for the switch on the gas range's exhaust fan, then turned his efforts toward opening the small kitchen window.

Virginia threw the pot holders on the floor, rubbing her burnt knuckles against her lips. "Grease fire," she gasped, trying to suck clean air into her lungs and moisture into her throat. "The steaks and the grill and the french fries." She was crying now: a mixture of anger and frustration sent tears cascading down her cheeks. "I just turned away for a second to make the salad and set the table." She coughed and sneezed, her diaphragm jerking spasmodically. She had hiccups! She kicked at the pan with her bare foot, nearly slipping on the salt-covered floor.

"Take it easy." Alex put a comforting arm around her sobbing shoulders. "Everything is under control, honey." He guided her through the rapidly dispersing smoke cloud into the living room. The alarm ceased its incessant clamoring as he settled her on his lap on the living room sofa.

"Oh, Alex, it was awful." Virginia was still hiccuping and crying. Her wet cheek snuggled into the curve of his neck while her hand clutched his shoulder. "Flames were shooting; hot grease splattered everywhere." The hiccups kept increasing. "Smoke . . . oh, the smoke, and then that alarm. I poured salt on everything." She gave one last long hiccup and literally collapsed against him.

"Darling, relax. It's all over," his languid voice crooned. He rocked her trembling body as if she were an injured child. "It probably won't ever happen again," Alex announced in a positive tone. "You're just going to have to be a little more careful." He pulled her chin up and kissed her tear-ravaged cheeks. "I never expected to have a 'flaming gourmet' on my hands."

Virginia sniffed audibly, her fingers toying with the luxuriant dark curls on his muscular chest. "Alex," she sniffed again, trying not to sound too whiny, "couldn't we order a pizza?"

He sighed and kissed her hard on the lips. "All right." He lifted her off his lap. "Let me get dressed." Alex looked through the archway into the kitchen and shook his head. "You've got quite a mess to clean up."

"I've decided to do this scientifically," Virginia told Diane. "This"—she lifted an orange-striped box—"is guaranteed to clean ground-in dirt. This"—she poured blue liquid on a shirt collar—"will remove neck stains. This"—she aimed a pump bottle at an ink smear—"will unspot clothes. And this"—she pulled a white sheet from a dispenser roll—"will eliminate static-cling and keep the clothes smelling fresh for weeks."

"Really?" Diane tossed a handful of all-purpose detergent into her washer, slammed the lid, and pushed in the coin holder. Leaning her denim-clad hip against the rapidly filling machine, she plucked a cigarette from her pink sweat-shirt pocket and hunted for a match. "I thought Connolly's picked up and delivered all your laundry."

"They're just doing the dry cleaning." Virginia carefully fit quarters into three machines, sighing with relief when they all began their wash cycles.

"Alex didn't like the way they did his shirts—too much starch. He said it was just as easy to come down here and throw our few things in the machine." She smiled brightly at Diane. "After all, it's not like we have to beat the clothes against a rock."

"Hmmm." Diane inhaled, made a perfect smoke ring, and watched it drift into invisibility among the copper pipes that ringed the basement laundry room. "I can think of more exciting ways to spend a Saturday." She cast Virginia a sidelong glance as they seated themselves on a pair of cold gray-metal folding chairs. "Where is your better half?"

"Alex is at the lab," Virginia explained, hunting through a pile of damp ancient issues of movie magazines for something more stimulating. "His laser experiments are giving him trouble, and he wanted to work on them." She gave up the search, tucking her own jean-covered legs Indian-style beneath her. "So," she smiled at Diane, "what have you been up to lately?"

"Just getting the rest of the Christmas presents to ship back home. I'm trying to wangle a couple of days off to go skiing during the holidays."

"That sounds like fun." She rolled up the sleeves on her green plaid shirt. "I'm really looking forward to Christmas this year," Virginia confessed, her blue eyes radiating excitement. "Never having a family to exchange presents, I've really gone overboard buying things for Alex and his folks and all the in-laws and nieces and nephews." She gave a contented sigh. "I was hoping we could fly to New Orleans so I could meet everyone, but since we're both outside consultants we don't get any extra time off."

Diane dropped her cigarette. Her blue tennis shoe drilled it into one of the many cracks in the concrete floor. "How much longer do you have at AVELCOMP?"

"Well . . ." Virginia scratched her cheek in thoughtful contemplation. "I don't really have that much more work. I'm hoping to wrap things up by the end of this week and then . . ." She paused, her gaze focusing back on the chugging washers. "Then maybe I can be a little more relaxed and concentrate on my wifely duties."

"Wifely duties?" Diane blinked.

"You know . . ." She gave a self-conscious laugh. "The cooking, the cleaning, the laundry, the cooking . . ."

"Especially the cooking." Diane cast her an amused glance. "How are you doing? Apartment-house gossip has it that your smoke alarm blew up because of overuse—"

"That's a rotten lie!" Virginia jumped in: "I disconnected the damn thing!" She looked at Diane, and they both burst out laughing. "Alex may be the only husband who's lost weight since getting married." She shook her head sadly. "In the past three weeks I've given every cut of meat third-degree burns; my pasta is either mush or brittle; vegetables soggy or still frozen in the middle; rice—even the minute variety—is like wallpaper paste. Alex said the chickens of America would commit suicide if they could see what I do to their eggs."

"He still won't let you serve any frozen dinners, huh?"

"No." Her blond ponytail swished back and forth. "Matter of principle, he said. All women are born cooks, it's in our genes."

"What a load of garbage!" Diane patted Virginia's arm. "How about taking one of those evening cooking classes?" she suggested, setting another cigarette on fire.

"I've been thinking about it." Virginia rubbed the back of her neck, surprised to find it damp with perspiration. "I just never realized how hard homemakers really work. They are truly domestic engineers." She turned serious. "You wage a never-ending battle against dirt and laundry. I never seem to get out of the kitchen—cooking and cleaning are self-perpetuating!" She thrust chapped hands under Diane's nose. "Look at this!" Then she hastily slid the rough red fingers between her legs. "Alex said it's a waste of water to use a dishwasher when there're only two of us.

"You know what gives me a royal pain," Virginia continued, working herself into a fine rage. "Those TV commercials depicting the working wife as 'superwoman.' " Her forefinger jabbed Diane's knee. "Those cheery little Madison Avenue creations come home from work with a big smile, dust and cook in their little Calvin Klein suits, read the kiddies a bedtime story, then turn into a sex goddess for hubby."

Virginia leaned back against the chair. "Now *that's* fantasy!"

"What's Alex doing while you're playing domestic engineer?" came Diane's caustic rejoinder.

Virginia stood up, jammed her thumb into her jeans pockets, and made an intent study of the rapidly turning wheels on the electric meters. "Well, he's . . ." She cleared her throat. "Alex is having a bit of a problem with that laser effect Glendale wants. He's been spending a lot of time trying to trace down errors."

"Can't you help?"

Can't I help? Virginia bit her lip. She had offered. She closed her eyes and remembered last Tuesday. She had made one small suggestion, and Alex had literally exploded. What did she know about his specialty? Was she the expert on everything? "No . . . no, I can't help Alex with this project." Her words were barely audible over the spinning washing machines.

"Ginger?" Diane's pert face peeked around her shoulder. "Is everything all right in Apartment Three-ten?"

"I love Alex." The words were said with sincere conviction. "I think once I get my projects cleared away, life will be easier." Virginia smiled at Diane, her cheeks suffusing with color. "You know, it's not easy living with someone. First, we're two different sexes, although that's the fun part." She laughed, her voice and manner growing lighter. "We were raised differently, opposite backgrounds; even our single lives weren't alike. But I'm a realist. It's going to take longer than three weeks to settle into a routine. It's not the 'happily ever after' you read about in books."

The washers spun to a halt, and both women proceeded to transfer their clean clothes to the driers. "Oh, look at this," Virginia groaned, holding up a shirt for Diane's inspection. "It went in white and came out dingy gray!"

"Don't worry." Diane sucked in her cheeks. "It'll match Alex's eyes."

CHAPTER NINE

Rain streamed from her hair, trickled in rivulets over her face to coldly meander down her neck and throat. Whoever said "it never rains in California" should be taken out and shot, Virginia decided. Her stockinged feet squished a squeaky tune inside water-logged leather oxfords as they followed a well-worn path from the elevator to her apartment door.

She groaned audibly when the knob refused to turn. First Nature's deluge, then an hour-long back-up on the freeway, then another half hour standing in line at the market, and now a locked door!

Lifting one knee to balance a grocery bag that had started to disintegrate the minute the clerk snapped it open, Virginia somehow managed to search her shoulder bag. Wet, numb fingers finally caught the metal key ring, and with a series of clumsy movements she struggled into the darkened apartment.

Virginia wiped her wet cheeks against the equally rain-soaked shoulders on her tan trench coat, while blindly groping her way toward the kitchen. The watermarked grocery sack grew more fragile with each step. She tried to hurry. Her foot twisted in her shoe; her arms slipped. The brown paper bag splintered from the bottom, sending a shower of boxes, cans, and other sundries bouncing and rolling across the carpet. "Damn!"

The end-table light snapped on, illuminating the living room. "What . . . who . . . what happened?" Alex's hoarse voice grated against her ears.

She looked from her sleepily blinking husband to the mess on the floor. Angry and exhausted, Virginia threw the rest of the bag on the carpet. "Didn't you hear me at the door?" Her voice was sharp, her features pinched in annoyance.

"I was sleeping." His words were muffled by a prodigious yawn. As Alex stretched his arms and legs the sports section slid off his chest. It found a home among the other tumbled newspapers littering the base of the sofa and coffee table.

"I'm glad someone was able to get a little rest," came her acidic rejoinder. Virginia shrugged off her raincoat and slipped off her shoes, placing them neatly in the entry closet.

Her mud-splattered beige pants and damp jade green blouse made her feel clammy and uncomfortable. She walked past Alex into the bathroom, returning a few minutes later in a warm, fleece-lined navy robe.

Alex watched Virginia curl into the far corner of the velour conversation pit, drying her hair with a towel.

"How did your meeting go in Glendale?"

"Fine." Her fingers combed through the wet blond strands. "It was a very long, long day. We worked through lunch." She closed her eyes. It was such a relief to have her end of the project finished. Virginia took a deep breath. She wanted to ask how his laser experiments went, but that was a sore subject. "Anything in the mail?"

He sat up, shaking the dullness from his mind. Crunching papers in the breast pocket of his brown knit shirt sounded intimidating to his ears. A muscle moved in his cheek. "Just a few bills, one of your trade magazines"—Alex flexed his broad shoulders —"and the usual junk mail."

Virginia focused on the empty mug, beer can, and cracker crumbs peppering the chrome-and-glass cocktail table. Her stomach felt welded to her backbone. "I'm starving," she stood up. "Let's eat. That casserole should be more than done."

"Casserole?"

She looked back over her shoulder. "I called to remind you. Didn't you put it in?" Her words sounded splintered.

"It slipped my mind." Alex scratched his head, his palms smoothing his thick dark hair back in place.

"Slipped your mind? Great!" Her hand slapped her hip. "It'll be another hour before it cooks."

"Let me get you a drink," he offered quickly, getting to his feet.

"No." The word was exhaled forcefully. "That'll just pique my appetite." She stooped to rescue a loaf of whole wheat bread from under the dining room table and headed into the kitchen. "I'll make a sandwich."

"Don't bother with anything for me," Alex called, bending to collect the fallen groceries. "I've already had a snack."

"So I see." Virginia sucked in her cheeks. Shaking her head, she stared around the galley kitchen. Cabinet doors gaped open; a wedge of cheddar sat crusting on the Formica counter surrounded by three knives and a box of crackers, which had fallen, leaving a snowfall of crumbs covering the floor. "You could have put things away, Alex." She stood framed in the archway, lips a thin pink ribbon against her pale complexion. "You could have remembered the casserole."

Alex looked from her angry-set features to the blue box of tampons in his hand. "Now I understand why you're so out of sorts." He gave her a consoling smile.

"Don't be ridiculous." She snatched the box from his fingers. "I've had my period every month since the age of eleven." Her voice was tight and brittle. "That's two hundred and twenty eight of them, and I have never ever been out of sorts!" She finished an octave higher.

"What I meant was," Alex continued in a soothing, languid tone, "you're probably just as upset as I am because you're not pregnant."

"Pregnant?" Her head reeled back, blue eyes blinking rapidly. "I never expected to be pregnant," Virginia pointed to a decorative blue jar on the spice rack. "That bottle marked 'One A Day' is not full of vitamins!"

His gray eyes narrowed. "I'd assumed your need for a contraceptive was over now that you're married."

She stared at him, her own eyes changed into icy chips. She didn't like his tone or his inference. "Well, you assumed wrong."

"We've never actually discussed having a family, but I know you want a baby. All women do."

"All women?" Virginia folded her arms across her chest. His generalities about the female sex were getting on her nerves. "Does it make me less a woman if I tell you I'm not the least bit interested in getting pregnant? Not now and not in the immediate future."

"You're not getting any younger and—"

"Listen, Alex." The words were tough. Her finger jabbed the air. "Women are not brood mares. We don't have a limited breeding season. Medical science has made great advancements, and women can have healthy children well into their forties."

"Are you going to cash your social security check to buy diapers and formula?" he taunted, his voice leaden with sarcasm.

"I may choose *never* to buy diapers or formula!"

Alex took a deep breath, cleared his throat, and gave her an encouraging smile. "Once you're settled in New Orleans, puttering around the house all day, you'll change your mind."

"Babies should not be created to ease boredom

and—" She stopped, tilting her head. "What do you mean New Orleans? I live in Florida."

"I have an apartment in New Orleans."

"I have a house in Cocoa Beach."

"My job is in New Orleans." Alex clearly enunciated each word. "Since you'll be quitting—"

"Quitting!" Virginia stared at him, her jaw dropping in amazement. "Where did you ever get the stupid idea that I would leave Briarcliff?"

His right eye began to twitch. "Are you proposing a shuttle marriage?"

Virginia sought to control her erratic breathing. "I don't know what I'm proposing." Her defiant gaze locked into his. "I only know I am not leaving Briarcliff. I am not abandoning my career."

"Well, just what is your next step, Dr. Farrell?" Alex leaned his hip against the dining room table. "The Nobel prize?" came his sardonic inquiry.

"And why not?" she retorted, moving closer to her husband. "Where is it written that I couldn't win the Nobel prize?"

Alex squared his shoulders, straightening, trying to use the extra few inches of his height to intimidate. "So that's it! Since you won the Science Medal, you think you're going to capture all the glory?" His lips thinned. "You know you've been impossible ever since you got that damn award!"

She swallowed hard. "I've been impossible?" Her voice was shrill. "Me?" Her balled fist hit her breastbone. "That damn award has nothing whatsoever to do with *who* has been impossible around this house."

"And what's that supposed to mean?" There was a deadliness to his words.

"I thought marriage was supposed to be a partnership. More than just love and commitment—equality too." Her bare foot tapped an angry tattoo. "A couple should share in both the benefits and the obligations of a marriage."

Virginia shook her head at him, wet strands stinging her cheeks. "But let me tell you something, Alex Braddock, you don't know the meaning of the word *share.* All you do is delegate!" A twinge of nausea twisted her stomach. "I'm getting a little sick and tired of your tried and true rules on what women should be and should do. Is this all carved in granite somewhere?"

She took a deep breath. "Alex, you are a male chauvinist—" She looked back toward the living room. Newspapers scattered everywhere, empty cans and glasses, crumbs, jacket tossed over one sofa, tie on another. She turned back to her husband and added, "Pig!"

Alex drew himself up with dignity. "Are you quite through?"

Virginia pushed up the wide sleeves of her robe. "I have not yet begun to fight!" she snapped. "I think it's high time we got a few things out in the open."

"Like what?"

"Well . . . well . . ." She licked her lips. "Let's start with the housework. 'We don't need a cleaning person,' you said. 'I'll help,' you said." Her head bandied cockily at him. "Help? Well, Alex, my definition of help and yours seem totally opposite.

"I don't call putting dirty clothes *on* the hamper instead of *in* the hamper a help. I don't call little teeny tiny bits of beard and shave cream all over the bathroom sink a help. I don't call tossing wadded-up socks under the bed and under the sofa a help. I don't call"—she stalked over to the couch, picked up his jacket, and snatched up his tie—"*this*"—she shook them at him—"a help."

"And do you think"—he ran his fingers over the narrow louvered blinds shading the dining room window, walked over, and shoved them against her nose—"dust is clean?" He smirked at her. "You hang your clothes on the doorknob or drape things over chairs."

"But in the end I pick them up. You don't!"

"I can't tell what's clean and what's dirty." Alex's lips twisted into a sneer. "All the laundry, either *in* or *out* of the hamper, is dingy!"

That rankled. "I'm not the one with the sweaty neck," Virginia replied waspishly, tossing his jacket and tie back on the sofa. "Why don't you try scrubbing out your own 'ring-around-the-collar'!"

"I'd love to, but unfortunately I'm usually too weak from hunger or hampered by acid indigestion to get much of anything done."

"I knew it." Her hands slapped her thighs. "I knew you'd make some nasty crack about my cooking."

"Cooking?" His laughter had a maniacal ring to it.

"That's what you call it. Cooking?" Alex gripped his stomach, his lips twisting into an exaggerated grimace. "I think poison would leave a more pleasant aftertaste than one of your meals."

"That's low," Virginia hissed. "I told you right from the beginning I was no Betty Crocker. I have tried my best. I have followed the recipes to the letter." She marched back to the kitchen. "Things would have been different. You could have made life easier for me if you hadn't been so damn fussy."

"Fussy?" He strode after her. "Do you call balking at eating ashes and cinders being fussy?"

"Yes, you're fussy!" she shouted. "Everything has to be made from scratch, and everything has to be fresh." Virginia yanked open the freezer and began slamming packages of frozen foods on the counter. "Stouffer's and Morton and Swanson's and Banquet weren't good enough for you!" She jeered and moved on to the cabinets. "Campbell's and Lipton weren't fresh enough." She dropped cans and tossed boxes at him. "I call that fussy!"

Her arm slashed amid the piled items, sending them exploding in different directions. Alex jumped clear of flying objects. "I don't give a damn whether plastic wrap clings better than aluminum foil. I couldn't care less whether Tide cleans better than liquid All. I have no desire to attend a Tupperware party. I am not Suzy Homemaker! Defrosting Sara Lee is my idea of gourmet!"

She took a deep breath, squared her shoulders, and moved into the dining room. "I've tried to do everything to please you, Alex, but our marriage can't be geared to just you and your needs." Virginia found her anger subsiding. Her voice, while still trembling, sounded much more rational. "You seem to have the impression that a man's home is his castle and he is king." She pushed her hair behind her ears. "Well, that was the day before yesterday. Traditional marriages are a thing of the past. Husbands have to do more, and right now you are doing less than minimal."

His eyes were twin slits of steel. "Oh, so I'm the bastard!" He pounded his chest like an angry gorilla. "I'm the one who's enslaving you?" Alex plunged his fists into the pocket of his brown trousers. "There are thousands . . . no . . . millions of women out there who manage to cook and clean and raise children and still hold down a job." He shook his head, wagging his finger at her. "But not you," he sneered. "You're too good for that."

"What you need," Virginia grated, her rage mushrooming with his sarcasm, "is one of those autoanimatronic Barbie dolls that whips up perfect soufflés, mops and shines in flowing chiffon, and turns into the perfect sexual playmate under the sheets."

"My mother did it all!" Alex shouted, his massive chest rising and falling in anger.

"Then, why don't you go home to your mother!" Virginia yelled back. "She's the only one who could tolerate such a hypocrite."

"I'm beginning to wonder why I ever married

you!" he growled, pacing back and forth like a caged lion.

"I didn't go into this marriage just to give you sex and maid service in exchange for support," she fumed, easily matching his angry strides with her long legs. "I don't need your support. I was always self-supporting. And I'm not a maid. It seems to me all we do have is good sex."

"As I recall," he interjected in a venomous tone, "I didn't have to marry you to get that."

Virginia caught her breath. The sheer malice of his words made her face flood with color. Her own tightly leashed rage made retaliation sweet. "As I recall, you were no virgin either."

They glared at each other. Bitter words hung in the air like invisible bricks, cemented together with destructive mortar. A wall had been constructed. Neither one attempted to climb over it.

Virginia tightened the belt on her robe. "My work at AVELCOMP is finished." She spoke in an odd, detached voice. "I am going back to my house in Florida and will await another assignment from Briarcliff."

Alex gave her a careless nod. "I've just got another few weeks left here myself." He walked over and picked up his jacket. "When I'm finished, I'm going home to New Orleans." He shoved his arms into tan corduroy sleeves. "Right now I think it would be better if I went to a hotel." He headed for the front door. "I'll pick up my things tomorrow."

"I won't be here."

"Fine." Alex stared at his hand, watching as five long fingers turned the brushed-gold doorknob. "You can file for divorce anytime you'd like." With that he walked out.

Virginia stared at the door for a long time, then her eyes wandered slowly around the apartment. The mess in the kitchen tumbled into the dining room and spread into the living room. Three rooms and two lives—all in an uproar.

The tabletop Christmas tree drew her like a magnet. She flicked a switch. Instantly tiny colored lights flared, then began blinking in a random pattern. Delicate hand-painted ornaments, candy canes, and white doves shimmered between swirls of gold garlands. She and Alex had selected everything with such care, with such love.

Beneath the tree were dozens of foil-wrapped packages, their tags warning: Do not open till Christmas. Christmas—it was only three days away. A holiday she had always hated. A holiday that signified togetherness and family and love.

Virginia swallowed the bitter lump that threatened to strangle her. She reached down and viciously yanked out the plug. Why should this year be any different?

"I really think you're making too much of your first little . . . um . . . misunderstanding," Diane repeated for the tenth time. As soon as Virginia turned her back, she scooped up three sweaters from the suitcase and quickly replaced them back in the bureau drawer.

"I saw that!" warned a sharp voice. Virginia snagged Diane's eyes in the mirror. Her head nodded toward the suitcase, watching as the clothes were reluctantly repacked.

"Husbands and wives fight all the time," Diane continued, flopping cross-legged on the edge of the bed. "You're making a big mistake by walking out." Her beige-tinted fingernails scratched confused little lines along the knees of her prewashed jeans.

"I didn't walk out," Virginia corrected matter-of-factly, "he did." She added a neat pile of lingerie to the suitcase. "Alex is very immature. I tried to have a nice quiet discussion, and he turned it into a . . . a . . . brawl."

Diane arched a blond brow, fluffing out her hair with a shake of her head. "It takes two to . . . brawl," she countered flippantly. "And from the looks of this apartment, I'd say you were both equally guilty."

"Say what you like," Virginia replied coldly. "I haven't one iota of guilt in me. I spoke the truth; Alex just didn't like what he heard."

"Maybe it was the way you said it," Diane suggested, her teeth clamped lightly around a cigarette while she searched the pockets of her khaki safari shirt for a match.

Virginia stuffed a few toiletries into the corners of the Pullman. "Relationships don't collapse under sledgehammer fights," she said in an even tone. "It's the little things that chip away the love. Twisting and turning it until love gets mixed with anger and turns to hate."

She looked down at her trembling hands, her tongue nervously tracing her lips. "It was like déjà vu," she whispered. Old memories whirled in her mind, making more than just her hands shake. "My career got in the way again. Alex resented my work, the award. He . . . he assumed I would give up everything. My house, my job, my hopes, my dreams. He didn't want to discuss it—he demanded it."

She nudged Diane over. "What's so wrong with a woman keeping her career once she's married?" Virginia asked, lackluster blue eyes staring into space as if searching for an answer. "I never flaunted my work at him. I never overpowered him." She blinked rapidly, trying to dam the tears burning beneath her lids. "Alex resents everything about me."

Diane slid a comforting arm around her shoulders. "Take it easy." One blond head leaned against another. "Sometimes men create their own anxieties, their own insecurities. I don't think Alex really resents you," she sighed, giving Virginia a quick hug. "Why don't you talk to him again?"

"No." Virginia shook her head, swallowing hard. "I'm not sure he even loves me. I think it was just infatuation and desire that got out of hand." She sniffed and wiped her eyes. "We should have just lived together. The novelty would have worn off soon enough, and the legalities would have been eliminated."

Virginia stood up. She felt calmer, more in control. "The best thing I can do is leave. Maybe I am smothering. Maybe that will always be the problem." She shrugged and went back to her packing. "Maybe I'm just fated to be alone."

Diane stared up at her friend's determined expression, then down at the suitcase again. She racked her mind for the right persuasive tone, the words that would make Virginia change her mind and stay. But even Diane found herself at a loss for something to say.

CHAPTER TEN

It was quite possibly the greatest tourist attraction in the world—Walt Disney World. In the last ten years host to over one hundred twenty-five million visitors. The Magic Kingdom was built on dreams and imagination: a one-hundred-acre theme park inviting guests to escape to six "lands," forty-five attractions, forty-one shops, and twenty-three various eating facilities.

Virginia was more than happy to cooperate with the Disney resort. She left reality and her blue Datsun in the Chip 'n' Dale parking lot, took a ferryboat to the main entrance gate, then boarded an old-fashioned steam train for a circular route around the entire Magic Kingdom.

The Walt Disney World Railroad chugged her back to Main Street, U.S.A. She settled into a horse-drawn trolley that clopped along the quiet boulevards of the turn-of-the-century village. Popcorn wagons and balloon vendors festooned the flower-lined square. There was a penny arcade with pinball machines dating back to the 1920s, emporiums, confectionery shops, and a movie house showing old Disney cartoons.

Along with everyone else aboard the trolley she yelled and waved to Mickey Mouse, Donald Duck, and Pinocchio, as that great trio of characters paraded among the crowds. A barbershop quartet harmonizing in front of their shop provided a group of Japanese tourists with the perfect opportunity to start clicking their cameras.

Virginia passed through the archway of Cinderella's Castle into Fantasyland. She took a cruise through hundreds of singing, dancing international dolls proclaiming, "It's a small world, after all." Then she went twenty thousand leagues under the sea in Captain Nemo's submarine, the *Nautilus.* She bypassed a half-dozen other rides to take the one-way Skyway to Tomorrowland.

The scenic journey high over the magic kingdom was breathtaking. The romantic spires of Cinderella's Castle soared into a perfect azure sky. It was hard to believe most of the country was being bombarded with snow and freezing temperatures. But the first week in February showed the tourists that Florida was truly the Sunshine State: her name meant "Feast of Flowers."

A revolutionary new transportation system, the WEDway People Mover, made traveling through Tomorrowland a pleasure. Virginia rode on a mission to Mars, took a "magic carpet round the world," courtesy of a 360-degree movie screen, then joined the throngs of screaming clench-eyed riders who soared through Space Mountain.

She piloted her own spacecraft on an aerial adventure and traced one hundred years of progress as presented by General Electric. It was a simple matter to go back in time: all you did was wish and head for Frontierland.

There the *Richard E. Irvin,* a Mississippi riverboat, provided a more relaxed, languid view of the unique dream created by the gifted hand of Walt Disney. Virginia hopped aboard a raft for a journey across the Rivers of America, anxious to explore the twisted caves on Tom Sawyer Island and rustic Fort Sam Clemens.

Lunch and entertainment went hand in hand at the Diamond Horseshoe Revue. Afterward Virginia tested her sharpshooting skills at the Shootin' Gallery, then caught a runaway mine train—Big Thunder Mountain Railroad.

Audioanimatronics abounded, from the foot-stomping, singing Country Bear Jamboree to the vivid, raucous buccaneers in the Pirates of the Caribbean. In the Hall of Presidents, Abraham Lincoln gave a dramatic recitation as all the other American presidents watched their spellbound audience with a realism that was astounding.

Virginia climbed through the Swiss Family Robinson's treehouse and finished her tour of Adventureland aboard a jungle cruise that was fraught with danger at every curve of the tropical river. An early-design fire engine brought her back to Main Street to the Epcot Preview Center. There she settled in the theater, along with several hundred invited guests, for a special sneak look at Walt Disney's greatest dream, which she had helped turn into reality.

Epcot—Experimental Prototype Community of Tomorrow—an eight-hundred-million-dollar project that was more than just entertainment. It was literally a center for prototype concepts. The Epcot Center theme, Spaceship Earth, illustrates how important to world survival communication has been in our past and how critical it is to our future.

Disney "imagineers" developed futuristic people-moving systems, more realistic special effects, all-new visual experiences, structural advancements, complex computer programming, and many other scientific achievements that entertain as well as show new frontiers of modern technology.

Epcot Center would be a showcase for the best ideas of industry, government, and academia.

The twenty-first century would truly begin at Epcot Center. Virginia found it difficult to contain her excitement; like everyone else she was on her feet applauding the newest wonder of the world.

Alex, however, remained seated. The blue-velour theater chair provided him with a perfect view of his wife. Virginia looked quite well, he thought. Much better than he, after forty days and forty nights of separation.

His gray eyes encompassed every detail of her feminine form. She was wearing a slim navy jump suit, which more than emphasized her long legs and well-proportioned curves. The overhead lighting haloed her shoulder-length hair, turning the soft waves into molten gold.

She was in a very animated discussion with three men, all of whom he recognized as fellow scientists. They seemed to be hanging on her every word—interrupting with a question, holding their breath for the answer only she could provide.

A tall dark-haired man whom Alex did not know came up and placed a red jacket over Virginia's shoulders. She looked back and smiled her thanks. Alex stood up. The stranger's hands had not moved. He didn't like that. After all, Virginia was still his wife.

"More Rabbit than scientist tonight?"

The instant wash of color that tinted her cheeks ebbed away quite rapidly, leaving her complexion a sallow mask. Virginia turned, her blue eyes meshed with those of her husband. "Hello." She had great difficulty voicing a coherent word.

Alex nodded, then shook hands with the three men he knew. Ignoring their puzzled expressions over his cryptic greeting, he turned his attention to the broad-shouldered stranger.

"This is Clayton York," Virginia supplied in a voice that felt shakier than it sounded. "He's with Briarcliff. Clay, this is Alex Braddock." She held her breath as the men exchanged the usual social amenities.

"If you gentlemen would excuse us . . ." Alex's hand clamped around her wrist. "I'm going to borrow the good doctor for a moment." Virginia mumbled an apology as Alex literally dragged her into a sheltered corner.

"Would it have been too embarrassing for you to introduce me as your husband?" came his sarcastic query.

She pulled her arm free, hastily rescuing the falling jacket. "As I recall, you walked out on that status and on me." Virginia responded, turning her attention back to the group milling inside the theater.

"As I recall, you didn't think it was such a great loss," Alex cracked, his voice clipped and brusque.

"Is there a point to this conversation?" Virginia inquired politely, raking her left hand through her hair. She refused to look at Alex. She didn't have to. She carried an indelible image of this complex man who was her husband in her mind for all time.

A glint of gold caught his attention. "No," Alex lied, jamming his own hands into the pockets of his navy trousers. "I'm sorry I took you away from your friends."

The odd inflection in his voice added to her confusion. Virginia turned to confront him but found he had moved away. She watched Alex disappear into the laughing, chattering crowd. The broad shoulders beneath his white fisherman knit sweater seemed uncharacteristically slumped. Or was she imagining that he could be hurting as much as she?

The switch from fantasy to reality had been a painful one. Even the wonders of Disney couldn't erase the memories that haunted her. Virginia left the theater, took the monorail back to the main gate, and bid a troubled good-bye to a land of dreams.

The BeeLine Expressway took her across the state. The crisp night air was perfumed by fragrant orange blossoms, the sky spangled with stars and a sliver of moon. Virginia wished she had been there when the first star had peeked through the inky cloak. But what would she have wished for? Alex. They seemed further apart than ever before.

Her hand groped along the dimly lit dashboard. She found the knob, and the radio sputtered to life with Barbara Mandrell's "Sleeping Single in a Double Bed." Virginia didn't need to be reminded that she was doing just that.

She punched in another station and found Bob Seger and the Silver Bullet Band's "Trying to Live My Life Without You." He was right, she conceded, a lump forming in her throat, that it was the hardest thing she'd ever had to do.

Viciously her forefinger stabbed the radio knob again, and the disc jockey announced Tammy Wynette's "D-I-V-O-R-C-E." Was that what Alex had wanted to discuss? She snapped the radio off. Her eyes were rapidly deploying tears of love, fear, pain, and anger.

The black stenciled letters on the mailbox gave Alex another cause for hope. It read Braddock, not Farrell. The wedding ring on Virginia's hand last night essentially made the same statement. For better or worse, till death us do part. He had never taken his ring off—he never would.

He parked the rented silver Zephyr behind a blue import. The beachside A-frame hadn't been difficult to find. It was an oddity among the sprawling Spanish-style homes. The chalet's rough-hewn cedar planking was weathered by salt and sun; towering palms vied with the high-peaked blue roof for a place in the sun, while banana and orange trees, studded with near-ripe fruit, dotted the lawn.

The unmistakable Atlantic roared its presence—the tangy salt air excited his lungs as gulls and pelicans watched his every step from a cloud-ribboned blue sky. Alex followed the poinsettia-lined walk to the front door. He was surprised to find how shaky his hand was, having made two attempts before he could zero in on the doorbell.

Virginia paled at the sight of him, the dark circles under her eyes matching the gray shadows that silhouetted his. She held the door open and motioned him inside. Her silence came from fear; anguish pinched her features. During the past six weeks she had filled the limbo of separation with dreams of hope. Would this confrontation shatter those dreams?

Alex could understand why she hadn't wanted to give up her house. It was sunny and inviting, full of plants and shells. Brown and beige leaf-print fabric covered the rattan sofa; wicker and glass accents were everywhere. His apartment was more like a hotel room. Furniture bought for comfort—just a place to sleep. Lately he hadn't been able to do even that.

The view from the triple French doors caught and held his attention. Sea oats and cacti banked downward, disappearing into soft white sand. Beyond lay the sea. Today its turbulent rolling breakers crashed an angry refrain against the beach.

Virginia loved the sea—Alex knew that. Somehow that gave him strength. She so easily accepted the ocean's moods. Wouldn't she be able to forgive him his?

Virginia perched on the edge of a rattan chair. She tried to put words together. "Can . . . can I get you something?" she finally blurted, wiping clammy palms against well-worn jeans.

"Yes."

She steeled herself. This would be it—words that could kill, deadlier than bullets. Divorce. Freedom. "Coffee, tea, a drink?" How inane, she thought, but she was scared to death.

Alex stood in front of her. His gray eyes searched her very soul. "What I really need is forgiveness, patience, understanding, and love." He dropped to his knees, his left hand groping for hers. Alex held his breath and waited.

Her fingers entwined with his. "You've always had the last," she whispered. Tears dribbled freely down her cheeks and splashed on their hands. "I think I need the others just as well."

He stood up, taking her with him. The warmth of her body reassured him, giving him the courage he so badly needed. "Virginia, I love you very much." He gently wiped her tear-ravaged face. "You do believe that?"

"Yes. Yes, I do, Alex." Her fingertips sought to smooth the tension from around his mouth. They pressed along the hollows of his cheeks to his eyes, only to find dampness there that matched her own. "I love you. I never stopped." Virginia pulled free of his embrace. "I am just so scared that love is not going to be enough for us."

She wrapped her arms tightly around her torso, trying to combat the numbness that invaded her green fleece-lined shirt. "The fight we had really skirted the issues. Important issues that have to be talked about."

Alex took a deep breath. "You're right. In fact, you were right about a lot of things." He gave her a wan smile and sat down on the chair she had vacated. "I will admit that I found it very difficult being married to such a successful woman, and yet that was one of the things that attracted me in the first place."

He ran a hand underneath the collar of his tan knit shirt. "I loved your independence, your talent, your abilities, and your creativity. Of course, it wasn't part of *my* life then," Alex sighed. He swallowed hard and continued.

"Jealousy is a very difficult emotion to put into words. I was even jealous last night when I saw Clayton York put his hands on you." His raised palm halted her interruption. "That's something I have to deal with. I have always been very vulnerable where you are concerned. It will take time, and that's why I need your patience and understanding.

"Virginia, you are just so damn good at what you do that it scares me." He looked down at his clenched fists. "In a way it emasculated me. I think that's why I suddenly turned into the consummate male chauvinist. I felt if I relegated you to the traditional woman's role, it would ease my own insecurities."

He gave her a wry smile. "This didn't help." Alex pulled a dog-eared envelope from the back pocket of his brown slacks. "It arrived in the mail the day we had our fight."

Virginia was surprised at the Briarcliff letterhead. It was a pleasant letter, brief and to the point. While Alex's qualifications were impeccable, they still fell short of Briarcliff's standards, and they could not offer him employment at the time.

She pulled up the ottoman and sat across from him. "I hope you won't take this the wrong way." She hesitated, with her even white teeth capturing her lower lip. "But I think this worked out for the best. Lots of companies have rules about husbands and wives working together, and maybe that would help us. If we had separate projects, we would both bring something different home at night. No one would invade the other's work territory."

Alex massaged his jaw. "That makes a lot of sense." He cleared his throat. "I have left SoLas. Disney offered me a job, and I took it."

"In California?"

He shook his head. "Right here at Epcot. They are building the largest nongovernmental array of solar collecting cells in the world. It will provide power for the ride vehicles in the Universe of Energy Center." Alex's knuckles gently fondled the sensitive cord on her neck. "Is there a chance that I might call this place home?"

Virginia turned her head. Her lips kissed the palm of his hand. "I would love it if you would." Then suddenly she stood up, pacing back and forth in agitation.

"Alex, I am still the same. I hate doing housework; laundry defeats me; and my cooking . . . well . . ." Her voice faltered.

"Listen, I am perfectly willing to let you run the house the way it's easiest for you." Alex smiled encouragingly, holding out his hand. "I should have been more cooperative. I should have helped set tables instead of turning them. Life would have been easier for both of us."

"We are lucky enough to be able to afford a cleaning person," she told him.

"I will certainly tidy up after myself," he inserted.

"We can have the laundry keep doing your shirts until they get them right," Virginia continued. He laughed and nodded, pulling her down onto his lap.

"About my cooking . . ." She snuggled against his chest, her fingernail teasing his earlobe. "I have been taking a course, and I'm doing much better." She peeked shyly through her lashes. "I built a microwave oven, and I am pleased to announce I have not vaporized a single meal."

Alex gaped at her. "You built a microwave?" She nodded. He gave a low chuckle, his fingers gently tugging her soft blond curls. "Most wives buy appliances. I am very fortunate in that my wife can build them." He looked at her inquiringly. "And what else have you been doing these past six weeks?"

"I did get a new assignment from Briarcliff," she sighed, toying with the buttons on his shirt. "It's really a paper one. They want a study on SQUIDS—superconducting quantum interference devices. I'll be doing labs down the road at NASA, writing reports. It should keep me busy for a year." Virginia burrowed her face against the warm curve of his neck. The spicy scent of his after-shave sent little ripples of longing flooding to every pore. "What have you been doing for the past month and a half?"

His hand slid beneath her shirt, kneading and caressing her silken skin. "It took me three of those six weeks to finish up at AVELCOMP. I ended up calling in another consultant. He made the same suggestion you did." Alex sighed and shook his head. "I'm glad you're not the type to say 'I told you so.' "

"Never," Virginia promised.

"Diane sends her best," he continued. "She really is one hell of a good friend. And"—Alex cast her a sidelong glance—"a wealth of information about you. I can understand why you're so reluctant to have any children." His voice was low and comforting. "You really had one hell of a childhood."

"I've been thinking about that a lot too." Virginia took a deep breath. "My biggest fear has always been what would happen to a baby if something should happen to us. Being raised in foster homes or institutions is not what I want for our child." She straightened slightly, her eyes intent. "But you've got such a wonderful family. I know they would love and raise our baby if something happened." Virginia smiled at him. "After we are more relaxed with each other, more secure, more confident, I think—" She stopped. "I *know* I'd love to have your baby."

"Our baby," Alex corrected. "And I am perfectly willing to feed and change and burp and share in raising a child."

Her blue eyes glittered a message that made him catch his breath. "Alex, please stay in my life forever."

"You just try to make me leave," he vowed, his voice savagely gentle. "From now on all arguments will be settled on the spot. No door slammings, no walking out—we never go to bed mad."

"I like that," she told him matter-of-factly, a smile curving her lips. "Especially the bed part."

"Oh, do you?" Alex returned silkily. "I assume there is a bedroom in this charming place."

"There certainly is." Her passion-glazed eyes hungrily caressed his face. Virginia leaned forward. Her chin fit neatly against his as her lips moved sensuously against his mouth. "But the sofa is much closer, and it's been such a long time."

Alex tugged her shirt free of her shoulders, tossed

it on the beige carpet, then deftly unhooked her bra. "I'm sure you won't mind if I pick all this up later," he murmured, his lips and tongue burning a path down the smooth curve of her throat.

Virginia cradled his dark head against her breasts. She sighed, her body trembling under waves of happiness. "Much, much later."

LOOK FOR NEXT MONTH'S CANDLELIGHT ECSTASY ROMANCES™